KILLERS

Reconstructed

NICOLE M. TAYLOR

EPIC
Press

Reconstructed
Killers

Written by Nicole M. Taylor

Copyright © 2017 by Abdo Consulting Group, Inc.

Published by EPIC Press™
PO Box 398166
Minneapolis, MN 55439

Cover design by Christina Doffing
Images for cover art obtained from iStockPhoto.com
Edited by Jennifer Skogen

LIBRARY OF CONGRESS CATALOGING-IN-PUBLICATION DATA

Names: Taylor, Nicole M., author.
Title: Reconstructed / by Nicole M. Taylor.
Description: Minneapolis, MN : EPIC Press, 2017. | Series: Killers
Summary: A college student is consumed by the unsolved disappearance of her brother a decade
    ago, and she launches her own investigation. But new evidence suggests that her brother's
    alleged killer might actually be nothing more than a scapegoat.
 Identifiers: LCCN 2016946207 | ISBN 9781680764895 (lib. bdg.) |
    ISBN 9781680765458 (ebook)
Subjects: LCSH: Cold cases (Criminal investigation)—Fiction. | Murderers—Fiction. |
    Murder—Investigation—Fiction. | Detective—Fiction. | Mystery and detective stories—
    Fiction. | Young adult fiction.
Classification: DDC [Fic]—dc23
LC record available at http://lccn.loc.gov/2016946207

EPIC
Press

EPICPRESS.COM

For all the Big Sisters in my life

1

The Boy With No Name

Last night, I dreamt of Isaiah again.

I didn't remember the dream—I never do—but I knew the familiar, queasy, low feeling I had upon waking. It was what I imagined an astronaut would feel when touching back down on terra firma after being up there amongst the stars. My gravity had shifted, but only for a little while, and now I had to come back down, to feel the ordinary weight of living again.

I'd only ever told one person about the dreams—my grandfather—who had suggested that maybe it was Isaiah's way of saying goodbye to me. If so,

he had been saying goodbye for ten years now and showed no signs of stopping. When I was fifteen and my grandfather died, I half-expected him to come visiting some night but he never did. It was only Isaiah who still had something to say to me, I suppose.

My phone said 3:22 a.m. I rolled over and fished my laptop out of my comforter. In the silvery glow of the laptop screen, I could see my roommate in the loft bed across from me, still asleep with half a dozen pillows piled on top of her head like some weird, soft cairn.

I propped the laptop up on my chest and flicked through my e-mail, discarding a number of promotional e-mails and some replies on a chain discussion in my sociology class. I saved but did not read an e-mail from my mother (the headline said "emergency," but I knew that was her code for "you haven't called in four days"). Finally, I clicked on a message from Detective Peterson at the police department. He had another project for me.

The projects had started about a year ago with an internship in the Mt. Clare police department offices. It had been pretty boring at first—turns out college sophomores aren't qualified to do much in a police precinct besides run things through the copier and hit up the Starbucks. I started redrawing the age-progressed posters of missing kids, mostly to combat my own boredom. Some of the original sketches were downright awful—wonky noses, weird teeth, eyes unevenly spaced. They hung helpless on the walls and cork boards, almost begging for someone to fix them.

I had always liked art, portraiture in particular. When I was still in high school, Dad even tried to convince me to go to art school rather than study criminology—probably the first time in history a parent tried to talk their kid *into* an arts degree. He thought criminal justice would be too much of an uphill climb for a black girl of modest means. "It'll be so hard," he told me, "in ways you won't even

expect." In the end, though, he had supported my decision because we both knew why I'd made it.

Eventually, my internship time became mostly devoted to drawing. I filled up a pad with the imagined adult faces of girls and boys who would never really grow up. One day, Detective Peterson noticed my work and suggested that I submit it for placement on the police department's cold case website. He was my supervisor, technically, but that mostly meant he had to take time out of his day to find busywork for me. I think he was a little relieved to find something for me to do that was actually useful. And my drawings *were* useful, or useful enough that he was still sending me case files on occasion, even though my internship had ended five months ago.

This one was labeled UID J-65921, and it wasn't an age-progression, but a reconstruction. "We have some morgue photos and a digital recon based on skull measurements," Peterson wrote, "but we are hoping you can give him a little more life. Work your magic."

I clicked the attached image and felt an incredible jolt of adrenaline, a shock and a fear that moved through me from my lungs to my fingertips. I managed not to cry out, but only barely.

It was Isaiah.

Or rather, it was a digital recreation of Isaiah, somewhat clumsily and impersonally done. But there were his big, almond-shaped eyes, long, girlish lashes, and his fine eyebrows that always made him look a little curious, a little bewildered. And there was his silly grin that made a deep dimple on one side of his mouth. It was the same way he looked in all my memories, all of my dreams.

I paused and forced myself to take a breath. It hurt as though I had been running hard, and I felt streaks of wetness on my cheeks. I closed my eyes and counted to thirty.

When I opened my eyes again, the boy on my computer screen seemed somehow different, though the image had surely not changed in any meaningful way. I noticed now that the boy actually had twin

dimples on either side of his mouth and that his lips were longer than Isaiah's. We both got Mom's small, round mouth—a rosebud mouth, she always called it. Most distinctly, though, the boy in the picture had a deformity on one ear. The top was pinched into a soft point instead of rounded like the other. It gave him the look of a disheveled baby elf.

At a second glance, the boy didn't really look much like Isaiah at all. Maybe it was the dim light, the lingering hangover from the dream, or just a moment of insanity. Isaiah was hardly the only lost little boy in the world.

I clicked the other attachments in the e-mail, a short dossier on the boy and some grim morgue photos, which someone had used to create the digital composite. There was always a little disparity, where someone had adapted or altered a real photo into a colorful digital painting, like a collage where the edges were always just a bit visible. It gave the image a strange unseemliness, like a creature that moves almost-but-not-quite like a person.

My ex-boyfriend, Sammy, loved Chinese vampire movies, and it reminded me a little of the way those monsters got around. It sounded funny to me at first—hopping vampires?—but actually seeing it was unsettling in a strange way, just like looking at this picture of a dead boy, his eyes digitally propped open, an artificial sweater drawn on him.

According to the dossier, the boy was estimated to be between nine and eleven years old, about sixty-five pounds, and fifty-three inches tall. He was well nourished, his teeth were in good repair, and he was originally discovered less than twenty-four hours after his death. He had languished, however, in the files of the Sherwin County Police Department, and they had just now gotten around to placing him on the state cold cases website.

The boy was not Isaiah. The morgue photos made it even clearer, and this boy was missing his appendix as well as being two inches taller and ten pounds heavier than my brother. But it was odd, the place where he was found. Sherwin County butted

right up against West Allertown, where I had grown up. The rest of the county was mostly farmland, edging up against the city, and I had always thought it was a little eerie how you could drive twenty, thirty minutes away from the apartment blocks and postage-stamp backyards of my home town and be in the middle of nowhere. The dark hills heaped up forever, and the long stretches of dirt road with trees crowding up over your head like a cathedral ceiling seemed to belong in some sort of fairytale. The place where I grew up was nowhere you'd ever catch Cinderella or Snow White hanging around.

It was a funny coincidence, though. If you took a boy from, say, West Allertown, which boasted the largest African-American community in the state, and you wanted to dump a body, you could do a lot worse than the lonely soybean fields of Sherwin County.

I clicked back over the dossier to look at the estimated date of death—on or around October 21st,

2001. Definitely not Isaiah then. Isaiah's killer was behind bars in October, awaiting his trial.

Across from me, my roommate's phone began trilling a little mechanical tune, and she stirred to swipe its screen. Alicia got up at 5:00 a.m. every day to swim laps. I missed a lot of things about competitive swimming but certainly not the early hours. Not that I was doing much better for myself; I must have been poring over this nameless boy for an hour and a half.

I shut my laptop with a snap. I had given enough time to the dead for one morning.

●   ●   ●

My Media and Crime seminar was my first and only class of the day at 10:30 a.m. in the Heapf Kiva all the way across campus. I deliberately didn't bring my laptop; the temptation to spend more time looking at the unknown boy's file was too great. Despite my attempts to busy myself with

something—anything—else, I had been preoccupied with thoughts of the case all morning.

At the front of the room, the professor had plugged his laptop into the projector, and he was working now to center the projected image on the hanging screen. Text too small to read and an indistinct face flickered against the nubbly terrain of the stone wall, before resolving itself upon the blank white square.

I felt as though I had swallowed an ice cube the wrong way, like something frozen was sticking inside of my chest. For the second time in the last five hours, I was confronted by a terrible memory, a face from my childhood. This time, it was not my brother, but the man who had killed him—who even now would deny him the simple dignity of a burial.

Darrin Wade Parris had grown out his hair in the last ten years. He was wearing it in small twists now, and it made him look younger, somehow. He looked like a college student himself, the kind with

a notebook full of poetry and a seat at every advocacy group meeting on campus. He was also wearing a small gold crucifix, and it glittered in the V that his prison-issued t-shirt made. Something about that cross created an overwhelming wave of disgust deep in my belly.

Is This The West Allertown Bogeyman? the title read, and the byline beneath it said, *Reporting by Melissa Clarence-Polk.*

"Darrin Wade Parris hasn't given an interview since his second appeal in 2003 failed," the professor said excitedly. "Our very own Melissa," he pointed at someone with a striped shirt and a soft bloom of naturally curly hair a few rows ahead of me, "is the first layperson to talk to him since then. And quite possibly the last, if his upcoming execution goes on as planned."

April 17th. Our family had been invited to send "a representative," but we'd ignored the letter.

"How many of you are familiar with the West Allertown Bogeyman Case?" the professor asked,

and several hands shot up. Mine did not. For a brief moment, I had wondered if he realized who I was and how I was connected to the case, but I quickly dismissed this notion. Our names had appeared in the papers once or twice, but Isaiah was one of an estimated twenty-three victims, when all was said and done. We were lost in the flood of the missing and the murdered.

Of course, why would my professor ever imagine that someone intimately connected to the case was right here in his classroom? After all, West Allertown was on the other side of the state, nearly six hours away. Plus, while the criminology major was a bit less monochromatic than some others on campus, there were still only four black students in the class, myself included, and one of them was an international student from France. When the professor looked out from his podium, he saw an eager sea of freckles and ruddy cheeks—kids from suburbs and little farm towns for whom the terrible autumn of

2000 was just a series of unpleasant headlines, if it was anything at all.

"Melissa," the professor continued, "Darrin Wade Parris has been notoriously resistant to any kind of media engagement. What made you approach him now?"

"I thought he might be desperate," Melissa said, her voice low and assured. "His execution date is approaching rapidly, and there's been almost no coverage of the movement to exonerate him. He needs the media now."

"Do you believe him?" another girl, across the room, asked. Melissa shrugged her shoulders.

"There were a lot of problems with that investigation. I think everyone knows that."

Their voices seemed small and far away, like talking with someone on a crappy cell phone. I couldn't look away from Parris's beneficent face, projected bigger than life on the screen. I had realized what it was that bothered me so much about his crucifix: it was nearly identical to the one that

Mama had worn all through his trial. When the jurors read out the "guilty" verdict, she had kissed it and sobbed so hard she nearly vomited.

Eventually, as the weeks turned into years and Parris showed no signs of ever disclosing what he had done with the bodies—with Isaiah's body— my mother stopped wearing the crucifix. I knew it was shut up in her little rosewood jewelry box, but if I hadn't known that, it would have been easy to imagine that he had somehow stolen it from her. Snatched it from the safety of her bedroom the same way he had snatched her son away.

"He was a clear scapegoat," someone else, a boy, just a few seats away, offered. "What'd they charge him with? Fifty-some murders? The police were clearing their docket."

"Twenty-three," I found myself saying.

"Yeah," the boy agreed quickly, apparently hearing nothing of my tone. "How many of those were actually the work of the Bogeyman, and how many were just . . . " He trailed off, but I knew what he

was leaving unsaid. How many were the simple attrition rate of young children of color living in the kind of neighborhood where his friendly, smiling parents wouldn't stop for red lights? How many were simply the "ordinary" disappearances and murders of little black kids?

The day Isaiah went missing, it was my mother who convinced us to call the police. Dad was holding on to a thread of hope that Isaiah was just lost, and we all had that needling, sickly feeling about calling the cops. In West Allertown, calling the police was a good way to turn a shit situation into a catastrophe. But Mom insisted. The officer didn't show up until the next afternoon. After listening to my mother's breathless panic, he told her that boys Isaiah's age went off on their own all the time. That he had probably gotten into some trouble and was afraid to come back to us.

"My son is not afraid of me," Mom said, with the tears leaking down her face to touch the edges of her gritted teeth.

"Then he'll come back soon," the officer said. And we never saw that man again.

"The forensics are unimpressive," Melissa agreed. "Except in the Manners' case."

Leesa and Shari Manners—the murders that had broken open the case and exposed all the bitter guts inside. Leesa was fifteen and her little sister Shari was just twelve; they were the children of Darrin Wade Parris's older half-sister. That was his big mistake, hunting amongst his own family members.

"Of course," the professor said in his plummy, playing-devil's-advocate voice, "those who believe Parris is guilty would argue that, since his incarceration, there have been no additional murders."

To this, Melissa offered only another shrug.

"I've always thought that he did it," a girl in the front row offered. *Always,* I snorted to myself. She had to be, what, nineteen? Maybe twenty? She would have been a little girl that fall, just like me. "People say that the killings were too different to all be the work of one person, but serial killers do

change and evolve. And there's always room for the occasional outlier."

The professor pointed at her excitedly. "Let's talk about that," he said. "Outliers."

* * *

After class, I returned to the boy in my e-mail, who was staring out at me with the same eerie expression, the same photoshopped smile. This time, I pored over the information that Detective Peterson had provided.

Isaiah was unusual in the canon of the West Allertown Bogeyman's victims, one of just a handful whose remains were never recovered. Mom had to fight to get him included on the list of the dead, citing his young age and his lack of any history of running away. There were plenty of others who didn't make the list, whose names rarely—if ever—appeared in the newspaper. Those who were simply allowed to go missing.

This unnamed boy, abandoned practically within spitting distance of West Allertown, could be one of those missing kids, unclaimed by a family but just as gone. I magnified the autopsy photos as much as I could and looked methodically over every inch of the boy's face, searching for something familiar. I was trying to decide if I had seen him, maybe, riding bikes in the street with the other boys, or in the halls at school, or even in the park at night, hanging with the bigger kids.

He had been beaten, according to the autopsy, something that was unusual but not unheard of amongst the Bogeyman's victims. His wounds had made his head puffy and soft, obscuring some of his features. That, along with the process of decay, which begins just as soon as a creature's heart beats its last beat, had certainly changed his appearance.

I began my sketch as I always did: with a plain pad of drawing paper from the grocery store. Later, I would transfer the image to my laptop and put the finishing touches on it there, but in the beginning,

I needed to feel the movement of the lines. I drew his big, slightly tilted eyes with a smooth, confident curve of my pencil. I shaded in his nose with short, dull strokes. I brought forth the point of his unusual ear with just the tip of my pencil. Light and fine, like someone had pinched off a piece of dough. I toned down the smile that the police artist had given him, leaving him with an expression more clever than joyful. I took away all his cuts and bruises, all the places where his flesh had been damaged and broken and left a quick and eager kid.

Before I finished, though, I sent an e-mail to Detective Peterson.

I think it would be a good idea to circulate the sketch around West Allertown. I believe he may be one of ours.

Peterson must have been sitting at his desk because he shot back a reply to me almost immediately.

Will do. Thought something like that. Between you, me, and the NSA, this was an organizational clusterfuck. Just found out the estimated death date for the kid is wrong in file, sub in August 21st, 2000.

August 21st, 2000. The day Isaiah went missing.

2

Andrea Ward

August 21st, 2000

Everywhere I go, Isaiah comes too. Like a shadow, except that he talks so much. Mama says that is what big sisters do, but I am barely a big sister at all. Auntie Selia calls us "Catholic twins" because I am only ten months older than Isaiah. At least we are not in the same class at school, but Isaiah loves nothing better than those two months out of the year when we are exactly the same age.

Maybe if we had been real twins, I would be able to like Isaiah as much as he likes me. I am Isaiah's best friend, his favorite person in the world. No matter what I do or say, he still wants to be wherever

I am. I don't know if I could love *anybody* that much. Though, if I was gonna, it would probably be Isaiah.

Little boys need their own friends; they can't be hanging around all time with older girls. I told Mama that but she said it was just fine. She said Isaiah will get friends of his own soon, and someday he won't want nothing to do with me. "And then you will wish for these days."

I was supposed to meet Shae and Kayla and Alana at the park to practice roller-skating. Mama had finally gotten me a pair of roller skates of my own (technically, I had asked for roller blades but she said they were too dangerous and too expensive). They were secondhand but she had buffed up the leather and put in brand new laces—pink with purple paw prints. You could hardly tell they weren't new, and they were better than the weird old kind that Kayla had that she just clipped on to her shoes.

But I couldn't bring Isaiah to the park, not after

last time. I had tried to bring him out to the Dairy Queen, and as soon as people saw I had my little brother hanging on my hand, they all of a sudden "just remembered" that they had to go to the mall, knowing full well that Mama didn't let us go to the mall alone.

There was only one thing more powerful than Isaiah's desire to tag along after me.

"How many packs will you buy?" he asked, bouncing along beside me in exaggerated hops that yanked my hand wildly back and forth.

"How much do they cost?" Ever since he discovered that weird cartoon, Isaiah had been obsessed with Pokémon. He begged for more cards every time Mom or Dad so much as stopped at a gas station. Dad had gotten so tired of it that he said Isaiah could only get a pack when his grades came in. That was not enough as far as Isaiah was concerned, but he knew better than to keep pestering. Dad didn't play; he could and would confiscate

every card Isaiah had if he felt like his own kid was nagging him.

"You're supposed to play with other people, right?" I had seen an advertisement in the library saying that they were opening their community room on weekends for kids to play all those different card games. It would be the perfect place to dump Isaiah for a few hours if I could get him to just let go of me for a little while.

"Y-e-e-es," Isaiah said reluctantly. "But I just like to have them. To look at them. I don't like to play."

What he really meant was that he couldn't find anyone to play with him. He had tried at first to get me or Mom to indulge him. We gave it a shot a few times, but he could tell that we weren't really that interested. Playing with kids in the neighborhood was out of the question; Isaiah would never just approach a strange kid and start a game. Or at least he wouldn't without a push.

The 7-Eleven was on the way to the park and just a few blocks around the corner from the library.

In the summer, Isaiah and I walked there all the time for Slurpees and, occasionally, for the secret packs of cigarettes that Dad didn't know Mom asked us to get.

Isaiah tugged on my hand, leading me over to the aisle that the store had devoted entirely to colorful monster cards of all varieties. Their foil packages shimmered in the sunlight from the big windows.

"How do you know which ones to pick?" I asked, holding up two identical packages.

"You just guess," Isaiah said. "I have lots of the same ones."

"Dad would be thrilled to hear that," I muttered.

"Can I get three?" Isaiah flipped through the shelf of cards, picking out packs with the surety of a gambler pulling a penny slot lever.

I turned over one of the packs to check out the price. "Four dollars! No way! You can get one." Mom and Dad only gave me five dollars a week for allowance and, more than once, they'd asked for it

back when the alternator on the car went or the price of propane went up.

"But there's only eight in a pack!" Isaiah wasn't a particularly whiney kid, but that just seemed to make it all the more annoying whenever he did get sulky.

"That's even worse! That's, like, fifty cents a card."

Behind me, someone laughed. I turned around to find a grown-up, though probably a young one. We had been so focused on the cards that neither of us had heard him come up behind us.

"They sure got a racket going, huh?" he said, looking me in the eye. He had warm eyes with crinkly edges and a goatee so neat and clean that I couldn't help but wonder if he'd just come here from the barber shop.

Isaiah was looking at me, waiting to follow my lead as usual. I nodded at the man but didn't say anything.

"How about I grab one of these for you?" the

man continued, reaching for one of the foil packages in Isaiah's hand. It occurred to me that the man didn't have anything else in his hands, not so much as a lotto ticket or a bottle of pop.

Isaiah let him take the foil package but couldn't look him in the eye, his natural shyness warring with his desire to get a free pack of cards.

"That's okay," I said in my loudest voice, grabbing up Isaiah's hand. "We gotta go anyway. Our mom is waiting in the car."

I pulled Isaiah up to the counter, digging folded bills out of my pocket as we went. I didn't look back to see if the man was watching us. The girl rung us up lazily while Isaiah fidgeted with the pack of cards, his chin tilted down so I couldn't see his eyes. I knew what he was thinking, the same thing he always thought whenever he sensed tension: that it was somehow his fault.

"You're okay," I reassured him as we headed out the door. "You didn't do nothing wrong."

I spared a quick glance behind us as we darted

through the parking lot. The man was still inside; I could see his silhouette in the big window, right where we left him. It occurred to me that all the time we had been in the store, I had never heard the electronic beep the door always made when someone came inside. Had that man been there all along?

"Just remember not to take anything from strangers," I told Isaiah. It was something our mother had told us both plenty of times. "Not food or toys or anything. No one is going to give you anything for free. Especially grown-ups. If a grown-up is offering you something, they're gonna want something from you."

"Want what?" Isaiah asked me as we turned down the block toward the library. It was different for boys, I realized. For more than a year now, I'd had men—grown men—yelling nasty things at me when I walked around outside. It happened when I was alone, when I was with friends, and one time when I was walking with Mom. She just went all stiff and cold. "Ignore it," she said. "Pretend you

can't hear them." I could though. I could hear them and I remembered everything they said.

"Nothing good," I told him, pushing open the library's big double doors and hustling him inside.

•   •   •

I left Isaiah at a big table in the back with three other boys about his age. Two of them had big binders full of cards in plastic sleeves, while the third had a stack as thick as my fist wrapped in a rubber band. I felt a little stir of regret. Isaiah's own collection was only about the size of a half-deck of cards. Maybe I should have bought him the extra packs?

Isaiah didn't seem to mind, though. He just sat down at the far end of the table and started opening the pack in his careful way. He liked to keep the foil as well. The other boys at the table eyed him but didn't say anything. I rubbed the back of his neck where his hair began to curl upwards.

"Be good," I said. "I'll be back in a couple hours."

He nodded but stayed quiet. I knew he still wanted to go with me, but we had made a deal and Isaiah was very good at keeping promises. I knocked on the library window as I passed by outside and pulled a stupid face at him. He smiled at me, but only a little, like he knew I wanted to see him smile more than he himself wanted to smile.

I couldn't seem to settle with it, that little smile he pasted on for my benefit. I decided that on the way back from the park I would stop back at the 7-Eleven and get him another pack of cards. He could not complain about that, and then we both would have a good afternoon.

In the park, Shae showed me how to do a new trick where you crouch way down and stick one leg out in front of you. As I predicted, Kayla was about pea green looking at my new white leather skates.

I stayed longer than I had meant. When Kayla said she had to get back before her mom got out of work, I realized that I'd been skating for almost three hours. It wasn't at all like being with Isaiah

when I would be so aware all the time of what we were supposed to be doing, and when we had to be back, and what Mom would say if I didn't look after him every second. Without him, I was so light that I nearly blew away in the breeze.

I wore my skates back to the 7-Eleven and to the library, figuring that it was surely faster than walking, and I rolled by the big library window, intending to hold up the newly purchased pack of cards and beckon Isaiah outside with it.

The library was especially bright in the creeping evening dark, and I could see there were now a bunch of kids at the long table, some of them split off into pairs, some clustered around individual players to watch them. What I didn't see, though, was Isaiah.

I got all the way to the children's section on my wheels before a librarian grabbed me by the elbow, turning us both around in an awkward do-si-do. "You can't wear those in here," she said, pointing at my skates.

I crouched down to untie them, close enough now to overhear the kids at the long table. Lots of sharp little voices, but again, I could not hear Isaiah amongst them. Isaiah was quiet, though. He was not the type of kid to push to the front and make himself heard.

I raced over to the table in my socks, earning myself another disapproving look from the librarian. Sure enough, Isaiah was nowhere to be found. Neither of the boys who had been there earlier in the afternoon was there now. I grabbed one girl about my own age and said, "Hey, did you see a little boy in a green t-shirt around here?"

She looked at me like I had spit right in her face. "No," she said, the same way she might have talked to a crazy person on the street.

"Did anyone see a little boy with a green t-shirt here? His name is Isaiah." A few of the kids looked up at me and shook their heads. The rest of them didn't even turn away from their game.

I was late, I knew, but it wasn't at all like Isaiah

to disobey me or anyone else for that matter. If I told him to stay at the library, he should have been right there when I got back. I moved through the children's section, checking all the small plastic tables and big bean-bag chairs. Maybe he had gotten bored with playing and had gone off to read?

But he wasn't in any of the nooks or any of the aisles. He wasn't using any of the computers in the big section in the front. He wasn't even hiding in the back where the grown-up books were kept.

"Excuse me," I said, approaching the same librarian who had stopped me earlier. "I'm looking for my brother. He's nine years old and he has a green sweater and jeans on. His name is Isaiah. He was supposed to be at the big table over there, but he's not there now."

She peered over at the table. "Kids have been back and forth all afternoon," she said. "I don't remember your brother specifically. Are you sure you were supposed to meet him here?"

I nodded because I suddenly found my throat

was painful and swollen. The librarian seemed as uncomfortable with my tears as I was. "Would you like to use the telephone? You can call your parents."

My "no" came out tiny and strangled. There was still a chance—a slim chance—that Isaiah had decided to meet me somewhere else. Maybe at the park or maybe even back at home.

It wasn't just punishment that I was afraid of, though I knew that my mother's wrath would be unholy. If I called my parents now, it would be almost like giving up in a way. If I called them and told them that Isaiah was lost, then that really would make him lost and I couldn't believe that. Not my brother.

No, Isaiah was just *misplaced*. He'd gotten confused or maybe even gotten mad at me for leaving him so long. He'd probably tried to come find me and we had just missed each other somehow. I rushed back to the park at top speed. By the time I got there, it was truly dark, but I searched all the benches and all the playground stuff anyway. I

didn't even let the high school kids gathered around the picnic tables to smoke intimidate me.

But Isaiah wasn't in any of those places.

There was nowhere left to go, then, except home. I turned the idea over and over in my head as I ran down the sidewalks towards our apartment building. Maybe Isaiah had been searching for me, too. Maybe we had been circling around one another, arriving at each new location just after the other person had left like something from an old comedy movie. Eventually, he would have figured what I figured—that he had to go home.

The closer I got to home, the more clearly I imagined him playing on the floor in the front room like nothing was wrong. It was so perfect in my head, that image, that I began to smile, even to laugh, despite myself. I was being so dumb, so panicky, and now I was going to go home and find him there, and I would be so mad I would tear a strip off him for wandering off. But I wouldn't really be all that mad, and he would be able to tell because he

was always able to tell when I was really mad and when I was just scared.

When I got home, Mom was already crying, the skin around her eyes puffed up soft and painful. My image of Isaiah on the rug with his action figures fell away in uncountable pieces. Already, I was grieving.

3

Visitation

I knew for a fact that Darrin Wade Parris would not accept a visit from me. Dad had tried about six years after the trial. Enough time, we thought, for Darrin to get bored of tormenting us and possibly reveal the location of Isaiah's body. The police had never pushed him very hard, never bothered to offer him a reduced sentence or other perks in exchange for that information. As far as the police were concerned, they had more than a dozen little bodies, and one more wasn't going to do anything for them.

Dad thought that maybe Parris would respond to a direct plea. Instead, all he ever got was silence.

After a while, Mom asked him to stop trying. She had heard from some of the other families of murdered children that Parris had ignored their overtures as well. It seemed that he wasn't seeing anyone, least of all the human wreckage left in the wake of his crimes.

I didn't know if, after more than ten years, Parris would remember my name or associate it with the little boy he took in the late summer of 2000, but I thought there was a good chance that he would. Thankfully, I knew at least one person that he would deign to see.

"I don't know," Melissa said slowly when I approached after class the next day. "I think that's illegal."

"It's frowned upon, but I don't think it's actually illegal."

Melissa was a few shades lighter than me and a few inches shorter. She had freckles and glasses and her hair was longer as well. We really didn't look anything alike, except that we were both young

black women. In my experience, though, that was often enough, especially if whoever was checking the IDs was white. Even in our Media and Criminology course, the professor had on multiple occasions switched up our papers, though from what I had read, our rhetorical styles were not at all similar.

"If you get caught, I'll be permanently barred from visiting Darrin and probably from visiting anyone else at that facility."

"I won't get caught. I'm going to go over Valentine's weekend." With the huge influx of spouses, girlfriends, boyfriends, and other assorted holiday visitors, I would have a good chance of flying under the radar. "I'll keep it quick, just a few questions and I'll be gone."

Melissa did not look convinced. "Why can't you just go under your own name? Doing the paperwork and the background check is a pain, but it really doesn't take that long."

For a long time after Isaiah died, there was never a question of whether or not to disclose what had

happened. Everyone at school knew who had been taken by the Bogeyman, and a lot of people had a connection to the case, if only second or third degree. "My cousin's best friend," "my neighbor's granddaughter," and, because of Dad, a lot of kids could say, "my English teacher's son."

In college, no one knew anything about me or Isaiah, which was, honestly, what I preferred. In my three years at Mt. Clare University, I hadn't told anyone what happened except for Sammy, and I'd been made to regret that. I realized I no longer even knew exactly how to say the words.

"Parris will know my name and he won't put me on his list. I'm . . . related to one of his victims." I felt like I was confessing some embarrassing personal flaw, and I shook my head a little, trying to brush the feeling off like a clinging cobweb.

I watched Melissa's eyes get huge. "No." Her voice had taken on a strict, almost lawyerly cadence. "No way. You can't go in there and confront him.

He'll ask to have you removed, and I'll get in so much trouble—"

"Whoa, whoa, no one said anything about confronting him. That's not . . . I have something else I want to ask him. Something important. But he'll never know who I am, I promise."

Melissa rolled her eyes skyward as though appealing to the Almighty for help. "Who did you lose?"

That wasn't the question I was expecting, and for a few seconds I said nothing at all. "My brother," I managed finally. "My little brother."

Melissa sighed at me. "You're not going to try to stab him or some shit, are you?"

"No, I'm not going to *stab* him. I have some questions for him, just like you."

Melissa hefted her backpack around to her chest and began digging in one of the front pockets. "I gotta warn you, you're probably going to be disappointed. I visited him six times and I never got him to say anything specific about any of the crimes." She produced a wallet from the backpack

and thumbed through it for her student ID. "I don't think he can give you what you're looking for."

Something had changed; a tenor of her voice shifted and became low and soothing. Something got soft in her eyes. It was the way I had expected her to look when I told her about Isaiah. It was the way everyone looked when I told them about Isaiah. It was like I had ceased to become a person to them and instead I was this open wound, painful to look at but demanding some gesture of sympathy.

When she handed me her ID, she squeezed my hand for good measure.

* * *

I hadn't been to the pool in almost three weeks. Partially it was school—I did have a lot of work to finish before the winter break—but it was also because of Sammy. I had some idea—some fear— that I was going walk in there and see him. It was where we met, bonding over our shared pull toward

the water, though both of us had stopped competing. For Sammy, it was a rotator cuff injury; for me it was a choice. Once I got to college, I couldn't afford to split my focus anymore and I knew where my attention had to be.

I liked to go in the mornings, as early as my ID would work on the door. It wasn't about having the lanes to myself—too many actual athletes like my roommate were already in attendance no matter how early I went—it was more about the darkness. If I got there before the sun started peeking through the windows I could slide into the water—underneath the water—a weightless world of cool darkness. It had all the comforts of sleep but also with a sense of being supported, being held.

It was always a little bit disorienting, pulling myself out of the water and away from that feeling of security, so it took me a minute to even realize that Sammy was standing there, high and dry at the edge of the pool. I guess he had been watching me run through some laps.

"Looking good," he said and I wasn't entirely sure if he meant my stroke or me in general. If it was the latter, then he was definitely lying. I hadn't been swimming as much, and I hadn't been eating right. Now I was seeing the effects. Since we broke up I'd gained about six pounds, and I was nursing a series of small pimples along my hairline.

Sammy looked the same, his hair a little bit longer, maybe.

"You here to blow off some steam?"

Sammy shook his head. "Training, actually. I talked to my physical therapist, and she thinks that I might be ready to get back into competition shape."

If I had still been his girlfriend, I might have cautioned him against the idea, pointing out how hard it would be to manage a real, serious practice schedule along with his coursework. Sammy was going into veterinary medicine, a surprisingly demanding major that took up a lot of his time and attention. But I wasn't Sammy's girlfriend anymore. I wasn't anyone to him, except maybe a fellow pool user.

"That's great," I said, reaching up under the rubbery edge of my swim cap and pulling it free. Sammy gave me that look of his, that sort of fond, soft look he had sometimes when I did something totally normal that he somehow found adorable.

"How are you?" he asked me so earnestly that between that and the look he gave me, I almost blurted out the whole story about Melissa and Darrin and my upcoming trip to the prison. I knew, though, that he would either try to talk me out of it or convince me to let him come along. I had told Sammy about Isaiah in a moment of maudlin drunken candor, and he immediately started pushing me to "share the burden," whatever that meant. Mostly therapy. It was a significant factor in our breakup, in fact. I didn't need a life coach or a psychoanalyst, and I didn't need to talk about Isaiah every damn day.

Wasn't it enough that I *thought* about him every day?

So I just smiled as hard as I could. "I'm great. Thinking about the future."

· · ·

Despite my big talk to Melissa and to Sammy, I was nervous when I walked into the state penitentiary. I had never been any kind of rebel or rule-breaker. Isaiah and I were alike in our knee-quaking terror of even the flimsiest authority figures—I once threw up out of anxiety after an assistant Sunday school teacher scolded me for running in the hallway after services—but, for Isaiah, I would pretend to be confident and brave. A leader.

Over the years, I actually did mellow to some degree and made space for the gray areas of life. I could drive ten miles over the speed limit or have a pot cookie at a house party without undue fear. Still, even the "wildest" things I'd ever done did not hold a candle to what I was about to do: lie to a cop's face while standing inside a prison. My stomach was

churning uncomfortably, and I tried not to let the sickly feeling show on my face.

I was relieved to see that I had guessed correctly about the timing. The processing area was already mostly full with a long line of folks holding heart-shaped balloons, large sparkly Valentine's cards and other assorted gifts. Some of them were toting babies or leading young children by the hand.

The line was moving fast, despite its size, and the inspections seemed pretty cursory. I had worn a wrap over my hair to disguise the length discrepancy and borrowed an old pair of my roommate's glasses. I clutched Melissa's ID so tightly that the edges cut red lines into my palms.

As requested, I carried no bags or packs, only my borrowed ID and a small file folder with some paperwork. A guard motioned me forward when it was my turn. He was chubby and young with his black hair gelled into drooping little points. He examined Melissa's ID with no great interest.

"Who are you here to see?" He didn't look at me.

"Darrin Wade Parris."

He looked up, his expression suddenly hawkish. "You made an appointment?"

I nodded, not trusting my voice. He half turned from me to consult a small pile of paperwork at his guard station. "Melissa Clarence-Polk?" he asked, as though he had not just read the name on my card.

I nodded again, tasting bitter bile in the back of my throat.

"You were here last month," he said, leafing through the papers. This did not appear to be a question, so I said nothing. He looked at me again, this time lifting the ID card up to compare it with my face. I resisted the urge to adjust my unnecessary glasses.

The silence had become almost painful when out of nowhere an angel—a baby angel with a blown-out diaper—came to my rescue. A few feet behind me, a baby in its mother's arms had started to cater-waul. Something greenish-yellow and reeking was dribbling down his leg, and he seemed as unhappy

about that as the rest of us. His ponytailed mother gave the guard an imploring look.

"Come on, come on, come on," he said, gesturing for me to step around the guard station where a female officer stood ready to pat me down. She worked quickly, smoothing her hands along the sides of my pants and sticking her fingers underneath my head wrap, leaving it slightly crooked.

"Take a seat," she said, gesturing toward a line of chairs built into a wall in front of a sad solo vending machine. "We'll call your name when he's ready."

I sat there for an unquantifiable amount of time, staring at the $3.50 bag of Doritos on the third row of the vending machine. *Damn*, I thought, *their shit's expensive.*

The people in the line behind me filed past me rapidly with no stopovers on the chairs. Melissa had warned me that seeing a prisoner on death row was a little bit more of a production than ordinary visitations. I fiddled with the small file folder they had

allowed me to bring, my drawing of the unnamed boy inside, along with several sheets of blank paper.

The guard had to call "my" name twice before I realized what was happening. "Sorry, I spaced out there." I was nervously over-explaining, but the guard just turned around before I could even get to her and started walking away without waiting to see if I was following. I jogged slightly to catch up with her as she led me down a hallway that reminded me of my middle school: the very same flecks of reflective mica in the floor, the very same industrial smell of bulk cleaner and unwashed bodies in the air.

She ushered me into a room where another guard was already waiting, staring at nothing in particular with his thumbs hooked into his belt. The room was divided down the middle by a wall, the top half clear glass and the lower half concrete. A series of jutting plastic barriers stuck out from the wall, creating something like a row of cubicles, only without the enclosing fourth wall.

Like cubicles, they offered only the illusion

of privacy. In addition to the guard, there were a handful of other people stationed at various booths carrying on low-toned conversations with indistinct figures on the other side of the glass.

"Fourth one down," the female guard said to me before she left me there.

As I approached the fourth booth, a shape on the other side of the glass began to resolve into a person. It was him. Darrin Wade Parris.

I felt as though the whole lower half of my body had gone liquid and insubstantial, as though I were treading water and doing it poorly. I flowed into the chair, rather than sat down.

At first, I didn't look up. I couldn't. I was sitting across from the man who had taken my brother. Who had, in a very real way, ruined my life. He had ruined my childhood for certain. Instead of looking at him, I took out the blank sheets of paper and a mechanical pencil.

I was startled by a loud rapping on the glass. I looked up automatically, only to find Parris pointing

toward the plastic phone mounted on the wall of the booth beside me. I picked it up with a firm, unquaking hand—and it took all of my strength to keep it steady. By the time I pressed the phone to my ear, it felt like I had just bench-pressed a Buick.

"You're not Melissa."

I hadn't heard his voice since that awful autumn and even then, he had barely spoken during the trial. "Yes, Judge" and "No, Judge," and "I plead not-guilty, Judge." And yet, his voice was terribly familiar to me, like a cousin or a distant uncle that I had known in childhood but hadn't seen in years.

"She couldn't come today." I tried to keep my voice light, mildly interested, non-accusatory. "She sent me in her place."

He didn't believe me, I could see it on his face. But he didn't push me.

He looked just the same as he had in Melissa's article header. Gold cross still winking at his throat. His face was warm and expectant.

"I just have a few follow-up questions." I shuffled

the blank papers as though there was something written on them. "Melissa said that last time you weren't interested in talking about the convictions"—he began to shake his head—"but we wanted to give you another chance to put forth your version of events."

"My version?" He smiled. "My 'version' is the same as it's ever been: I didn't have nothing to do with those murders. Sorry, girl, that's all I got for you."

I sighed into the phone. "No one thinks you're getting a stay of execution. Your appeals are all gone. This profile is the only thing keeping your name in anyone's mouth. The state is going to kill you in six weeks, and your only statement about the fourteen children you allegedly murdered is gonna be 'no comment'? Is that really what you want to leave behind when you go?"

His face clouded over immediately. He leaned into the glass as if to get a better look at me. I did not move or flinch away because I could imagine

how much that would delight him. "You look familiar to me," he said. I shrugged in what I hoped was a careless way. He just kept looking at me through the glass. I thought of my sixth-grade class trip to the aquarium, how I had gotten fixed in front of the octopus tank, watching its rapid, roiling movements and the sensuous ripples of its many arms.

"There's been a new development in the case." As soon as I said the words, I wanted to bite them back. Detective Peterson would tear me a few new assholes if he found out I was sharing confidential police information with a convicted murderer. Plus, there was still no proof at all that the unnamed boy actually was connected to the other child murders. Yet, it was the only thing that I could think to say. Darrin had all the cards in this game, and he'd had them ever since that day in August.

Something must have worked because he sat back slightly and his face became more neutral. "Yeah?" he said, in the same the way someone might react

to news that the grocery store was having a sale on avocados.

"Yeah. They found another body. Actually, they found him back in 2000, but the paperwork got lost. Looks like someone's gonna have to update your Wikipedia page."

He smiled a sliver of healthy white teeth. For years whenever I thought of Parris in prison, I imagined a broken thing, prematurely aged, wasting away. But he barely looked as though ten weeks had passed since Isaiah disappeared, let alone ten years. His skin was clear and bright, his arms were well-muscled, his posture was easy and comfortable as though we were meeting across a desk or a dinner table, instead of a sheet of impenetrable bulletproof glass.

"Melissa didn't send you, did she?" He was still smiling, but I was sure my expression had transformed into something altogether rawer.

I held up my sketch of the unnamed boy. This time, I couldn't stop my hands from shaking. The

boy's face quivered gently in the space between us. "Do you recognize him? Do you know his name?"

"I recognize you. You were at my trial."

I lowered the picture of the unnamed boy. He stared up at me, smiling his fruitless smile.

"Yeah," Parris said softly, though I had remained silent. "I remember you. You were wearing that shirt with the strawberries on it, with the real thin straps. What were those shirts called? With the real thin straps?"

"Spaghetti straps," I murmured. I remembered that shirt. Mom had bought it for me at the beginning of summer and I must have worn it nearly every day. By the time Parris went to trial, it was really too cold for the top, but I had insisted, telling my mother, "Everyone watches us. I want to look nice."

That was one of those afternoons when Mom went into her bedroom and closed all the curtains and shut the door.

"You looked good," he offered. His smile had become wolfish.

"I was eleven," I snapped. "About the same age as your niece when you murdered her."

"You don't know shit about that," he snapped back, just as angry, just as uncontrolled. I felt a swoop of adrenaline in my throat. Now, it was me who leaned up close to the glass.

"I know you like to mess around with little kids. Can't hack it with women your own age, huh?"

"She was grown," he insisted. "Anyone who looked at her would tell you that. From behind, she looked eighteen, nineteen or so. And she acted like it. She knew exactly what she was doing."

Interesting then that the older girl, Leesa, had shown no signs of sexual assault or a history of molestation. Apparently, once a girl got some hair on her legs or a learner's permit, she was no longer a good prospect for *Mr. Parris.*

"What about my brother? He was small for his

age, barely ten years old, and I can tell you for a fact that he didn't look any older than that."

Parris wrinkled up his forehead and gave me a quizzical sneer. "I never met your brother."

"I didn't even tell you which one he was."

"Don't matter. I never met any of them." He leaned heavily on one elbow until his forehead was nearly touching the glass. I could see a faint sheen on his skin—was he sweating? The room wasn't warm but I had a feeling that lots of things were different on his side of the glass. "I told all of you before, I didn't have nothing to do with those little boys."

"So what are you then?" I realized as I said it that I was talking way too loud, and I lowered my voice to a hissing whisper. "Just another innocent brother? A victim of the prison industrial complex?" The words were acid, and they almost seemed to burn the skin of my mouth on their way out.

"I'm not a homo," he said and I had the sense

that, were we not physically separated, he would have taken a swing at me.

"And Isaiah wasn't a man," I shot back. "He was a child."

"Isaiah? Isaiah Ward?"

I was a little surprised that he would remember the name after all these years. There were, after all, so many names.

"I already told your mother that I didn't touch that boy. She believed me. Why don't you?"

I gripped the phone tighter, pressing it so close against my ear that it began to ache. "What are you talking about?"

"Your mom. She used to come here regular a few years back, asking me all about her boy, and where I was that spring. I told her what I'm telling you: I never looked sexually at a boy in my life. I'm one hundred percent straight and that year, I was driving a cab. If they had those GPS tracker things back then, I'd be a free man right now." There was a weary edge in his voice and for the first time some

of his bravado seemed to have sloughed off, leaving only exhaustion and despair behind.

"They found your hair and skin under Leesa's nails," I said, and I couldn't help but feel like someone tossed from a shipwreck, latching on to anything that might keep me afloat. Except instead of a piece of wood or a life preserver, I was clinging tightly to the gory details of a young girl's murder.

There was an awful coldness in Darrin Parris. Gone was the easy charmer I had seen in Melissa's photographs, and gone also was the smug devil he'd played at the beginning of our conversation. Now he looked like a created thing, like an intricately detailed doll or automaton that someone had spent hours crafting lovingly. But when it came time to animate it, instead of a heart or a soul, they had instead inserted a stone.

"Yeah, but did they find it anywhere else?" he challenged.

"You confessed." I remembered the exact words as reported by both the newspapers and the police.

They were so clear, he might as well have carved them into my skin: *I snatched them. I fucked them. I killed them so they wouldn't tell.*

"Do you know how long nineteen hours is?" Before I could answer, he lifted his hand to silence me. "I know you probably think you do. That's a couple nights' sleep or a long road trip or whatever. But you don't know what it's like to *feel* every second. To know when each and every minute passes. The time starts to weigh on you, like a coat made of lead. Nineteen hours. That's how long they questioned me for that first night. By the end, they could have shown me a picture of Mickey Mouse and I woulda swore I decapitated the motherfucker myself. And that was the *first* night."

I knew from hundreds of case files and my own common sense that not everyone who confessed to a crime actually did it, but I had never doubted Darrin's confession. Maybe I hadn't wanted to.

"I'm not a good person," Parris said, and for the first time we were in total agreement. "But there's

folks in here who did way worse shit than I did. Real depraved. And they'll be out in ten, twelve years." He stared right at me through the glass. I finally saw the fear in his eyes that I had expected to see from the beginning. "I'm gonna die in here over something some other person did. If they gotta kill me, it at least should be for my own shit."

4

Darrin Wade Parris

August 21st, 2000

I took Arlington to Cross to Van Buren to get around the traffic downtown and make time for one more fare before I had to pick Shari up after her summer school.

It was a good thing to be doing, looking after the girls while Michelle was getting her shit together. Ever since her man died, she'd been struggling, looking after two kids on her own and trying to get by on her receptionist's salary. It didn't surprise no one that her oldest, Leesa, was running wild, slutting it up every chance she got. Leesa didn't even bother to sneak out anymore; she'd leave right in front of

her mother's eyes, and if Michelle tried to do anything, Leesa would go after her, scratching and throwing girly punches.

Michelle forgot her own raising. If she had ever lifted her hand to our parents when we were coming up, Daddy woulda put her in the hospital. But it wasn't all Michelle's fault. Most women have a soft touch. That was why kids needed a man around to show them the way.

Leesa was probably a lost cause. She'd been given too much leeway for too long. But Shari . . . Shari was a good girl. Shari still did as she was told.

On Arlington, a group of school kids started crossing against the light. I laid on my horn heavy to give them a scare. A few of them jumped in a satisfying way, and one girl looked right at me.

She was right in the middle of the crosswalk, backpack hanging off one shoulder. She was about Shari's age or a little younger and when she moved, the sunlight shone in the space between her legs. She

was wearing just a little pair of blue shorts and she had her hair up in a high ponytail on her head.

Even through the windshield, I could tell that she wasn't wearing makeup the way so many girls did these days, painting their eyes glitter-pink and their lips that weird chalky beige color. She looked like a good girl, a clean girl whose mom had taught her right.

She was right at that perfect age, too, that fulcrum point before everything went to shit. She had that long, lean body and she moved with just a little uncertainty, as though it were all new to her. Give her a few years—hell, give her a few months—and she'd discover the unearned power that came from just having a pussy.

About halfway across the street, she paused again, turning to look right at me with those big, clear eyes, and I felt a jolt of energy cut right through me, straight to my groin. It was so bright and immediate and strong that it almost hurt, and I clenched up my stomach and put my hands on the wheel.

That sort of thinking—that sort of feeling—
was exactly what had gotten me in trouble back in
Chicago and I couldn't go down that road again.
Not here in the place where I grew up.

Still, that girl with her big eyes and her long, thin
legs stayed with me, like a ghostly passenger, all the
way across town.

• • •

The girl in Chicago had been slightly younger and
not nearly as beautiful. She was chunky, in fact. The
kind of kid who wore sweaters that didn't fit all year
'round. Any other day, I wouldn't have even looked
her way.

Daddy always told us that there was no future in
boozing. He'd been a hellion in his younger days,
and he had that special fervor that only the reformed
have. Once, in high school he caught me with liquor
on my breath after a night out, and I thought he
was gonna kill me. Fifteen years old and nearly taller

than him, it was the last beating he ever gave me and the worst.

Michelle looked after me when Mama refused—it wasn't the first time I'd been caught sneaking liquor. "You never learn," she told me every time she hovered over me, dabbing Neosporin on the sore welts all over my legs and ass.

She was right and Daddy was too. Drinking never brought me anything good. It felt like comfort, like slipping through a door into another world where everything was softer and lighter, and all my movements, all my actions, didn't seem to land so heavily. But it was a false comfort, a betrayer.

I was very, very drunk that day in Chicago when I saw the girl.

Daddy had been dying slowly for a long time. Lung cancer. He managed to quit the drinking but couldn't let go of the cigs. The doctor told me it would be any day now. I had taken him back to the little shitbox apartment we shared, and all day I sat

there and listened to the air making its long, slow, terrible journey into his lungs.

I knew he was close to the end because he didn't say nothing, and his face didn't change when I sat there drinking gin right in front of him.

Daddy never saw the girl, thank God in heaven. I did it all in my car, and when I was done, I came back to him and didn't say nothing. He lived another few hours, and I was sound asleep when he passed. I know Michelle thought I left Chicago to get away from the sad memories, and that was true, after a fashion.

I never meant any of it. I was nearly blind from drinking. Every time I touched her, it felt like something that was happening on another planet, like I was controlling the arms of some toy or robot. I was watching from outside myself, marveling at how much effort it took to make my fingers move and my hands clench.

●　●　●

I got to Shari's school just as it was letting out. She had just moved to the middle school because she had been held back a grade; that's why I had Michelle enroll her in summer school. The teacher said she wanted to test her for some sort of learning problem, but I put a stop to that. "They'll put her in the class with the retarded kids," I told Michelle, "and she'll never come out again. If she needs extra help, I'll help her."

Shari wasn't slow, she just needed someone to keep her on track. Every once in a while, when she really couldn't get something, I'd just jot it in for her. She was only in the fifth grade, it wasn't no life or death thing. She'd been doing much better since I come into the picture, and as far as I knew, no one was talking about testing her anymore. There was nothing worse for a kid than being different.

She was waiting just where I told her to—on the benches in front of where the buses pulled up. There was someone, a little boy, hovering next to her like an unwanted fly who couldn't find the

open window. I rolled to a stop in front of her and honked the horn. "Get over here!" I shouted. I was annoyed to see that the boy followed her over to the car.

"Uncle Darrin, can Kie get a ride with us?" Shari leaned into the passenger seat, looking up at me through her long, dark lashes. She knew that I couldn't say no to her when she gave me that look. Even the good ones grew up, I supposed, and figured out how to push men's buttons.

"Sure," I said, unlocking the backseat so they could climb inside. The boy—Kie—looked at me in the rearview mirror, looked me right in my reflected eyes. I knew exactly what he was after and it made me sick. It was never too early for those boys, once they got the scent of it in their nose.

"What'd you do to your ear?" I asked him as we pulled out into traffic. The right one was twisted up weirdly on the top, like someone had given him a hard pinch.

"Nothing," he said, still looking right at me. "It was like that when I was born."

"Can I go out tonight, Uncle Darrin?" Shari asked me. She knew what I was going to say, I could tell by the soft tone in her voice. She shouldn't have even asked and I could guess who had put her up to it.

"School night," I grunted. "Where does your friend need to go?"

In the back, the boy's eyes flicked from Shari to me and back. She half turned to look at him and shook her head, like she was offering him a consolation. "You can drop me at the library," he said. "I can walk from there."

Damn right he could. He could pay a fare like anyone else if he wanted a taxi service.

The library wasn't too far from the school. I stopped outside the big front windows. When the boy leaned forward to unbuckle his seatbelt, I heard Shari whispering to him. "I'm sorry," she said. "Maybe another time."

Kie flashed her the kind of grin that made good girls want to go out on school nights. "No problem, girl," he said. "More for the rest of us."

"Thanks for the ride," he said, looking again at the rearview mirror. He had an appraising stare, sizing me up as the competition. " . . . Mr. Darrin," he drawled. Nasty little scrounger.

We were silent together in the car after I dropped the boy. Shari knew she had done wrong and she was waiting for me to light into her. She didn't even try to turn on the radio like she would usually.

I let her sit in it, taking the long way back to the house. Finally, after fifteen minutes, I told her, "I don't want you hanging around that little shit."

She nodded, staring down at her folded hands on her lap.

"He's trying to get up your skirt, and we don't need any more of that in our house, do we?"

She shook her head.

"Do we?" I insisted.

"No, sir," she answered in her smallest voice.

The long way around went out to a big open lot. In my day, it had been a baseball field and us kids used to stay out there until it got dark, just playing pick-up games. It was a good spot, quiet and nice for thinking.

I pulled us up there and stopped in the shadow of a stand of trees. Just across the lot, there were two big apartment complexes and a supermarket, but right there, it felt like nowhere. Wild nature creeping over the things humans had made.

I turned the car off and looked at her. "You want to stay a good girl, don't you?" I asked her. She did; we both knew it.

She nodded, still staring down at her hands. I reached over and took one of them. So little! The purple polish on her nails was chipped. "You've been a good girl, haven't you?"

"Yes, sir," the words got caught on the way out of her mouth, but then she swept her eyelashes up and looked right at me, and I thought again of the girl in the crosswalk.

"Then you won't mind if I check?" I asked, even though I knew she would not. She never did.

•   •   •

Leesa was eating macaroni and cheese out of the pot when we got home, which just about figured. These days, we never saw her except when she needed food or money. As soon as we walked in the door, she glared at me, just the evilest look that she could muster.

"Where have you been?" she asked in that awful snot tone that made we want to show her the back of my hand.

"Picking up your sister, 'cause nobody else around here is going to lift a goddamned finger." I yanked the pot out of her hand and slammed it back on the stove. She stood there with the fork in one hand, just waiting to do something, *craving* it. I looked right in her eyes, daring her. Even Michelle couldn't fault me if she took the first swing.

"School ended an hour ago," she sneered. "You pick her up on a bicycle?"

She had no shame, getting after me like that, all *where you been? Who with?* In my own goddamn house, like I was the teenager and she was the grown-up.

I took her hard by the upper arm, digging my fingers into the flesh that spilled up over her too-tight bra strap. She howled and twisted, trying to get away from me and yelling, "Ow! Ow! Ow!" but I didn't know who she was shouting for because Michelle was at work, and Shari was at the table, reading in her math textbook just like she was supposed to.

"I don't answer to you," I said, while she struggled. She started slapping at me with her free hand and I cracked her a good one across her face. She stopped and just looked at me with big, dumb eyes like no one had ever hit her before.

"Mom never shoulda brought you here," she said. There was nothing but pure hate in her voice. That

girl was a lost cause. I don't think there's a man alive who could straighten her out now.

* * *

Before the girl in Chicago, I'd been talking with other girls in the complex but none of them were very interesting. Dull-eyed and too old, their legs fell open at the first soft word. But they were easy, and it's hard to say no to something that's not going to cost you much effort. Like finding money on the ground.

I don't think I ever in my life got my first choice. I don't think I ever looked at a girl and thought "that's the one," and then made it happen. Instead, I got the scraps. The girl in Chicago knew she was scraps. That's why she let me buy her things, let me take her into my car, let me do everything to her. She couldn't have expected much more from the world.

It was almost a mercy, when you really thought about it.

She wasn't anything like the girl I'd seen in the crosswalk, who probably got told every day that she was pretty, and she was special, and she was something more than all the other girls. She had that kind of look, that radiance that some girls get when they know that everyone loves them, and they don't ever expect anything to be otherwise.

The first girl I ever fooled around with was a little like that. She was my babysitter's daughter, and she had hair like a cloud and she smiled all the time. Maybe she was the closest I got to my first choice? But I never even really got to start anything with her because Mama found us one day in the laundry room, crouched on the concrete floor.

Mama went easy on me, all things considered. She could have told Daddy and that would have meant the end of everything. Instead, she took care of it herself.

After she shooed away the babysitter's daughter,

she took me into our bathroom and made me strip down to just my underwear. I was shaking so hard she had to help me undo my jeans. I was eight.

While I was doing that, she turned the shower on and wrenched the handle all the way over to the hot side, as far as it would go. I could see steam rising up in curls from the shower head when she told me, "Get your ass in there."

I did, as slow as I could manage, and I tried to cling to the edges of the tub where the water barely touched but Mama wasn't having that. "Get right under there," she said, pushing me into the burning spray of water. I knew it would be worse if I defied her, so I did as I was told, even though every stream of water on my skin seemed to stab at me.

"Scrub," she demanded then, handing me a brillo pad from the kitchen, the kind with the blue soap already caked into it. I started to rub it gently on my chest but she yanked my hand down to my groin wordlessly.

It hurt so much. There were places where my

skin wore away entirely, leaving just shiny, slick patches that were agony to touch. Every time I changed my clothes for the next three days, I would tear away any new healing and it would all start over again.

Mama, who washed my underwear and saw for herself the blood and bits of skin and yellowish fluid, said that it would teach me. And it did.

I decided then that I wasn't ever going to get caught. Not by Mama, not by Daddy or Michelle or the teachers at school or the police. That's why I couldn't let that Chicago girl leave my car.

So I was extra cautious that night when I saw Leesa, her face fat and already bruising from my slap, in Shari's room. She was sitting on the girl's bed talking low, probably so I couldn't hear them. I didn't like it. Just looking at the two of them, lit up with the reddish light from Shari's bedside lamp, I got that sick feeling in my bones the same way I always did whenever I looked crossways at a girl growing up. Like I was gonna turn around and find

Mama standing there, though she'd been dead and gone now for six years.

"What are you doing?" I demanded from the doorway and Leesa looked up at me, a snake ready to spit poison.

"Reading her a bedtime story." She said it like I was the stupidest person she had ever met. She lifted up a paperback book, previously hidden in her lap. It had a mouse on the cover.

I looked at Shari, who had buried herself under the covers, so only the top of her face—her nose on up—was visible.

"Keep it short," I said. "You know she has to get up early for school tomorrow."

"I know," Leesa snapped back. "She's my sister. I know what she needs."

I left them then, went to fold out the sofa in the living room where I slept. It clearly wasn't no use, fighting with Leesa. Not tonight at least, with Michelle coming home any minute. A mother works

hard for her family, and she is right to expect some peace and quiet when she comes home.

But that didn't mean I was gonna forget Leesa's smart mouth, or the way she looked at me. She had no right, no right at all to treat me like I was scum when I hadn't done anything bad. I was taking care of Shari when no one else could. I was protecting her from the world. There was nothing wrong with me and Shari, and I wasn't going to let anyone tell me otherwise, least of all some uppity little bitch who thought she knew everything because she was fifteen and the world hadn't shown her any different yet.

One way or another, that girl was going to grow up real quick.

5

Home

For nearly half my life I had believed that I knew, more or less, what happened to my brother that day in August. There were gaps, of course (how did he encounter Parris? And where was his body now?) but I knew from the many other stories the general shape and contour of my brother's final hours. Now, though, that old knowledge seemed insufficient—insubstantial, even.

I had never looked closely at the deaths of Leesa and Shari Manners. I had always assumed that they were basically akin to all the other murders, except that this time Parris had gotten sloppy. He struck

too close to home and left something of himself behind for the police to find.

That was certainly the narrative I saw in a lot of old articles online written during the trial. If I went back further, though, back to just after Leesa and Shari were found dead, some discrepancies started to emerge.

Nearly all the Bogeyman's victims were strangled with something, some sort of cord or wire that the police never found. On three occasions, victims were shot but always with a large-caliber rifle and always in the back of the head—an oddly orderly type of murder for the Bogeyman.

By contrast, Leesa and Shari were both shot multiple times with a small-caliber handgun. Their hands were tied with shoelaces and the extension cord from a table lamp, but he did not strangle them.

The other victims were scrupulously clean. Some people had even speculated that the Bogeyman clipped the children's fingernails to prevent exactly

the kind of evidence that convicted Darrin Wade Parris. Shari and Leesa had not been in any way "prepared." They had been dumped in the city cemetery almost exactly as they had been when he killed them. His only real attempt at diverting the police was to wrap Leesa in a shower curtain and tuck Shari into a large camouflage cooler.

The more I looked at the Manners' murders, the less they seemed to have in common with the other deaths. Other than the fact that Leesa and Shari were black children from the West Allertown neighborhood, there was little to connect them to the Bogeyman at all.

The articles I read about the case seemed to lead only to more articles, and there did seem to be something to the idea that a whole lot of crimes had been laid on the Bogeyman's doorstep with some pretty dubious evidence. The Manners sisters weren't the only cases that stood out in terms of victimology, method of murder, and body disposal. During Parris's trial, much

had been made of the fourteen children between the ages of six and fourteen that he was accused of murdering. At one point, the prosecution had even brought in a big board with all of their pictures on it. Isaiah was there in the last row, smiling in the too-big sweater that Mom had told him he would grow into.

They hadn't mentioned the other nine people Parris was convicted of killing. That number included a couple of adult women who didn't seem to fit in with the rest of the Bogeyman's roster, as well as one young couple shot outside the West Allertown mall. That seemed much more likely to be the work of an unstable ex than a serial killer of children. There was even a toddler on the list—two-year-old Michai Langston, who was suffocated and hidden in the forest with his Thomas the Tank Engine sheet wrapped around his head. Why would the Bogeyman develop a sudden interest in babies that never showed up again?

I knew that criminal profiling was hardly an

exact science, and a number of big name profilers had commented specifically on this case, saying that the Bogeyman had an "evolving" victim selection process, and that many serial killers changed their targets for various reasons. Still, it seemed an incredible array of human depravity. Could one person possibly contain all these different permutations of awfulness?

Was it possible that Darrin Parris was, more or less, telling the truth? That he was *a* bogeyman, a monster for Shari and for Leesa, but not Isaiah's monster? That, apparently, was what my mother had come to believe.

I called my mother once every three days. It was a spacing that I had worked out over three years of trial and error. I rode a perilous line; any longer and my mother's panic instincts would kick in. Any shorter and I would drown in her misery.

I took summer classes and part-time jobs to ensure that I would only be able to come home once or twice a year. Even just those short stays were

almost unbearable, putting me instantly back in the worst of my high school days. Everything had gotten worse since Dad passed. It was a stroke, a sudden and brutal loss, but at least we knew what happened to him. At least I got to kiss him goodbye, even if it was at his funeral. It was a lot for a family to weather, and we responded by . . . not being much of a family anymore.

Going home was like cocooning myself in a thick, tangled mess of blankets. At first it feels warm, even comforting to be held so close. Then, as all the space around you begins to fill up with heat and moisture, and your own breath turns back on you, it begins to feel like a prison, like a death sentence, and you begin to panic and tear at everything around you, everything holding you in, just to breathe the cold air again.

College was my refuge. The idea of going back home filled me with sickly unease, but my computer could only take me so far. It could not tell me why my mother had reversed her position on

Darrin Wade Parris. Or why she had kept it a secret from me.

Christmas was a long way off, though, and I didn't have a car. This was partially because of the cost, but mostly it was something else I could lean on when she asked me to come home more often. I rode my bike around campus, but that obviously wouldn't work for a six-hour drive. Besides, even if I could carve enough out of my budget for a train ticket, the nearest station was a half hour north of here, and who would pick me up on the other end? Mom didn't drive, and in the last year, she had even started getting her groceries delivered.

There was one person who could help, though I could not imagine why he ever would.

Sammy picked up right away, even though it was the middle of the afternoon. He always liked to front-load his classes on Fridays so he could start partying in the afternoon if he wanted. Today, it sounded like he'd already gotten high. He couldn't

even get out a "hello" without a little stoner chuckle in the middle.

I felt a flash of an old, proprietary annoyance. Who was I to get mad at him for smoking weed on his own time? What, was he supposed to be sober and available at all times in case the girl who dumped him needed a favor?

"Hey Sammy. It's Andrea."

"I know your voice," he said sweetly, teasingly.

"I was wondering if you could . . . help me out?" He could probably hear the cringe in my voice. I couldn't believe that I was having this awkward conversation with someone I didn't want to talk to at all, so I could go somewhere I didn't want to go and see someone I didn't want to see.

"Sure."

"Don't agree yet. You don't know what I'm going to ask." I was slipping into lecture-mode. Sammy always seemed to bring it out in me.

"Whatever," he said, cheerfully careless. I almost smiled. As much as I got after him for being

irresponsible or impulsive, that was what I had liked about Sammy, that ease he had.

"I need to borrow your car."

"Okay," he said, "but you're driving. I'm a little baked." *You don't say?*

"I was just gonna . . . go . . . alone?"

"Nah," he said. "You drive. I'll navigate." I wanted to say that sounded like a terrible idea, but I had to admit that the notion of having company along for this trip wasn't completely terrible.

"Wait . . . where are we going again?" he asked.

◦ ◦ ◦

The drive to West Allertown was six hours, and Sammy was sober by about hour four.

"Your mom's not in trouble, is she?" he asked, watching the fast food places flit past with a certain familiar longing.

"No." No more than usual, at least. Mom had always been . . . fragile. She took a major hit when

Isaiah disappeared, and then when Dad died she just lost it. Whatever thing it was inside a person that makes them get up every morning and strive toward something, she didn't have any of it left. I used to want to scream at her. I would even fantasize about hitting her, just raining slaps down on her. I realized eventually that would all be a waste—a waste of feeling, a waste of kinetic energy. Like hating a stone.

Sammy and I dated for almost a year, but I had never taken him to the apartment I grew up in. I went to his house in New Jersey a few times and spent Thanksgiving and Christmas in his parents' meticulously decorated guest room. They were the first people I knew who had a "townhouse."

Sammy's mother was a chemist and his father was a podiatrist. They were immigrants from Taiwan who made good; they had produced a pediatric surgeon daughter, a financial analyst son, and Sammy, who grew his hair long, regularly smelled like weed, and brought home a black girl for the holidays. No

one was more surprised than me when his mother actually took to me.

"You understand," she would say approvingly to me, though I never knew exactly what I was supposed to have understood.

"She just likes anyone who kicks my ass," Sammy said dismissively when I brought this up, but I could tell that he was glad, in his way, that his mother approved of me.

Mom had never met any of my boyfriends.

"You want me to wait in the car?" Sammy asked when we pulled up in front of the apartment building. If he had tried to come with me, and I had to tell him to stay, I wouldn't have even considered doing anything else, but the fact of him asking jolted me into thinking about it. It was dark by the time we arrived, and I could see Mom's forward facing window. No light there.

"No," I said, "come along."

• • •

I knocked more out of politeness than because I thought it would actually do anything. Mom was always home and never answered the door. She was either hiding or sleeping, and at this hour, my guess was sleeping.

After waiting a minute, I let myself in with my spare key and gestured toward the sofa in the front room. "Wait here," I told Sammy. "I'll go get her."

The apartment was blue-black and the only sound was the dull, distant buzz of a television set. Mom couldn't sleep without a television going. It used to drive Dad crazy. I found her in the bed they used to share; she was in the same housecoat she'd had nearly all my life and sleeping soundly. Looking at her with her face all still and peaceful, I felt a little stirring of love for her. Maybe this was the only way I could love her, when she was still and silent and dreaming.

When I was little, my mom was the best mom in the world. She was the kind who would let you

skip school and take you to the lake on the first warm day of spring. She was the sort who got you up in the middle of the night to make cookies and insisted on stopping the car and getting out to search every time she saw a stray cat or dog running in the dark.

It wasn't until I got older that I started to realize that other moms didn't do those things, and for good reasons. That for every wild, creative, joyful moment, there were those dark hours when it seemed to hurt her just to move and breathe and be alive. That the things I loved about her were part of the things that made it impossible for her to keep a job, that kept us poor, that meant I had to be responsible for my brother.

Now, though, I could look at her and pretend for a few seconds at least that she wasn't hurting so badly all of the time.

"Mom," I said, leaning down to touch her shoulder. Her eyelids snapped open and I saw panic in

her eyes before it dissolved into relief and then settled into her habitual wounded look.

"Andrea? What are you doing here? You scared me half to death!" She sat up, reaching for the light and I sat down on the bed beside her. She stretched out her arms to me, and I hugged her dutifully. Like all her hugs, it lasted just a little bit longer than was comfortable.

"I'm sorry I scared you, Mom," I said when we finally broke apart, "but I need to talk to you about some things."

She watched me with a wary look, like she knew what I was getting at.

"I went to see Darrin Wade Parris in lockup." I watched the expressions flit across her face: shock, disappointment, a little bit of fear, and finally a dull resignation.

"Well," she sighed, "get up and I'll make you a coffee."

• • •

"Oh. Hello," Mom said, mildly curious upon seeing Sammy sprawled on her sofa. He gave her a cheerful wave.

"That's my friend Sammy, Mom," I said, trying to steer her back toward the kitchen before she could start trying to feed him year-old cookies she was always saving "for good." Sammy didn't try to follow us into the kitchen, and I felt a swell of gratitude toward him.

"I never told your father this," she started, pulling the coffee can out of the cupboard. It was the equivalent of her saying that she'd never told *anyone.* "I used to drive up to the prison when he was at work. Sometimes I only just got home before he did. That's part of why I stopped going."

"Part?" I moved to the other cupboard and grabbed three coffee cups, painstakingly avoiding the one covered in Shakespeare verses. That was Dad's.

Mom measured out the coffee grains with a painful exactitude, like she was defusing a nuclear

bomb. "I don't think I was going for him, really. I realized that, eventually. He didn't have the answers I needed."

"About Isaiah?"

The coffee burred and hummed, the red light glowing. In the living room, Sammy had found the remote. He turned on the TV and pretended to be very invested in a late-night infomercial.

Mom sat down across from me. I hadn't noticed before how pained all her movements looked. It was as though she was an arthritic old woman, though she wasn't even fifty yet. "About anything. He was just a . . . a warped thing. And he couldn't tell me what happened to my baby."

"So you believe him? That he didn't do it?"

Her eyes were so big, they seemed to contain all the sadness in the world. She nodded. In the living room, a man with a booming voice was offering to buy my gold. "How can you be sure?" I asked.

"No one is sure of anything, Andrea. But he told me things that made me think he was being honest

with me." I got the sense that she didn't want to tell me exactly what these "things" were. Even though I spent my days studying murder and misery, she still thought there was something fragile in me that would flinch away from Parris's confessions.

I reached out quickly before I could talk myself out of it and pressed my hand over hers. "You can say it," I told her. "I promise you I have heard worse."

Mom gave me an uncharacteristically sharp look. "No, you've *read* about worse. Maybe seen a film strip or something. But it's different when the person is sitting right there in front of you, telling you how they took a life."

"He admitted a crime to you?" He had gotten close to copping to his nieces' murders with me, came up right to the edge of it, but he had ultimately backed away. If my mother had managed to get a confession out of him—a real one—that was huge.

"He did," she said. "A girl in Chicago the year

before it all started. He said that the police found her body but never knew who did it. After he told me, I went to the library and got on the Internet." My mother had yet to join 98 percent of Americans and get an Internet connection in her house. "And everything he told me was true. There was an eleven-year-old girl they found, wrapped up in a shower curtain just like that poor little one he killed here."

"Maybe he . . . read about a crime in the paper and told you about it." I knew I was stretching. There was still some part of me that didn't want to face the idea that Darrin Parris wasn't my brother's murderer.

"Maybe," Mom allowed but I could see that she was agreeing more for my benefit than because she thought I might actually be right. "But then I found out about the others."

"Others?"

"Before Isaiah, before any of them, a handful of kids went missing in Sherwin County. When they

showed back up again they were all clean, clothes washed, even. Just like here."

I couldn't believe that. She had to have misinterpreted something. There was no way that police wouldn't have connected something like that to the rash of disappearances in West Allertown. There was no way I wouldn't have heard about it, if not in the papers at the time, then in my studies at school.

"There were three of them," Mom said. "But they were all little white kids and no one thought that a killer would switch like that. Switch neighborhoods, switch races. Then they found Darrin and it seemed even less likely that they were done by the same person."

Sherwin County was rural and extremely white. A young black man couldn't get a cup of coffee in most parts of the county without being noticed, let alone lure a bunch of school kids away from their parents. It was a familiar argument; lots of folk had argued the reverse after Parris was arrested. None of those lost children would have gone with

an unfamiliar white man, so it had to be someone from the neighborhood. If it was someone from West Allertown, then the Sherwin County murders couldn't be connected. It all fit together if your first priority was convicting Darrin Wade Parris.

"He couldn't have done those murders," Mom continued. "He was still in Chicago then and everyone said as much. After I found out about the other kids, I just . . . knew. In my heart. I knew he wasn't the one." Unshed tears pushed at the edges of her eyes and she swallowed painfully.

"Mama, why didn't you tell me?"

She smiled, but so sadly, and allowed her tears to fall and make shining tracks across her cheeks. "Tell you what, baby girl? That the man who took your brother away from us *wasn't* rotting in a jail cell? That he was free to walk around and do as he pleases? That Isaiah is lost to us, and the monster that stole him will never know a day of punishment for it? I couldn't tell you that."

I thought so often of my mother as a burden—on

me, on Dad, on everyone. Rarely had I stopped to consider the burdens that she herself bore, carrying them so uncomplainingly that we never even knew they were there. "I'm sorry," I said, surprised to find that my voice was thick, as though I had a cold coming on. "I'm sorry for that, Mama."

There was a moment when I might have hugged her. It would have been easy to get up from my chair and put my arms around her. But I didn't move and she didn't move, and the moment drifted away from the both of us.

"He sent me a couple of letters," Mom offered. "After I stopped coming. I sent one or two back but I stopped pretty quickly. I didn't need that."

"When was this?"

"Around the time you were graduating from high school." I had been busy then, hustling to finish scholarship applications and narrow down my school choices. I was also spending as much time as I could away from the house, which was always dark and cool like a cave. It felt like if I stayed there too

long, parts of me would start to atrophy from lack of use. Like those fish deep underground that slowly evolve into blindness. And all that time, my mother was carrying on a correspondence with a murderer.

"Your cross," I said suddenly. The end of high school was also about the time she stopped wearing it. I didn't know exactly when it happened; all I knew was that one day I came home and realized her throat had been bare for a while.

"I gave it up," she admitted. "Sent it to him with my last letter. I figured it might still . . . have something for him. Because it didn't have anything for me."

I couldn't blame her for that. She had prayed so long and hard for Isaiah to come home, and then for his killer to be convicted, and finally, pitifully, for his bones at least to come back to her. And the answer, each and every time, had been a resounding "no."

"Did you ever tell the police?" I asked. "About the girl in Chicago or the white kids?"

Mom laughed, so sad, like she was laughing at herself for being an awful fool. "Every time I tried to get in touch with the police, they'd send me to some different person who'd want to know my name and my case number and all my information all over again. You remember how it was. They just didn't want to talk to us parents."

"And as soon as I so much as mentioned Sherwin County, it would all shut down. They'd hustle me off the phone, tell me that wasn't *relevant*. They treated me like a crazy person and I get enough of that elsewhere."

I felt a little blossom of shame. She was talking about me. How I put on my kid gloves for her, and how I took important tasks out of her hands, sure that she would only fuck them up. How I never shared any part of my life with her.

"Baby?" Her face brightened. "Would your boyfriend like some coffee?"

*   *   *

The plan had been to drive back home that night. It would be tough but doable, and I would be back in time for my morning class.

"C'mon," Sammy argued, "you're exhausted. You're not safe to drive, and I know you have unexcused absences you can use."

He was right. I had a perfect attendance record for that class and I could afford to miss a session. Mom stood behind him at the sink, dishcloth clenched in her hands and her body all tense, like she was trying not to let herself hope.

"Okay," I said and Mom's face lit up in a way I hadn't seen in a long time. Since before Dad passed, maybe.

My room was exactly the way I had left it— swimming medals tacked to cork board and collages made from faces in magazines. Our apartment was bigger than a lot of other units, but it was still only two bedrooms, which meant Isaiah and I had to share a room. After he died, I spent years trying to scrub out or paper over the remains of him. I'd

done my job well. The only things left of him in the room were a cardboard box full of clothes in the closet and the bunk bed we shared. Mom and Dad never had the money to get a new bed, and the bunk bed itself had been a hand-me-down from Dad's brother. I slept there until I left home, my feet hanging off the end.

"You can sleep on the sofa," I told Sammy, who was even taller than me.

"Nah," he stretched out on the lower bunk looking like he'd been born there. While we visited with Mom, I had been watching him, looking for any sign of discomfort or disgust at the surroundings. Everything here was clean but old, cheap and small. He didn't seem to care, though. "Did you do that?" he pointed across the room at my desk where I'd hung up a few drawings. The one he was gesturing toward was a portrait of Dad I'd probably done when I was fifteen or sixteen.

"Yeah." It wasn't my best work; some of the textures were off, especially on his mustache, but I

had gotten something. Something in his expression, something familiar but indescribable, something that was gone entirely from his still face in the funeral home. *I should have done more drawings of him*, I thought. *I should have done dozens of them.*

"You're really talented," Sammy said appreciatively. "You still draw?"

I thought about my unfinished sketch of the nameless boy. "Sometimes," I said. "In special cases."

      •   •   •

I woke up to my cellphone vibrating the pocket of my jeans, which I had not bothered to remove before crawling into bed. I managed to answer the phone before the other person hung up and heard silence for a moment before a robotic voice informed me that "an inmate at the Mt. Clare State Penitentiary would like to call you collect. Will you accept the charges?"

"Uh-huh," I mumbled before adding a more decisive "yes."

After another moment, the line gave a warm crackle, and I heard Darrin Parris's voice, curiously closer than it had sounded through the similar phone at the prison. "Andrea?" he asked. "Andrea Ward?"

I turned my face into the pillow in the hopes of muffling my conversation. Less than a foot below me, Sammy let off a series soft snores. "How did you get this number?"

"Melissa gave it to me. I remembered something after our talk, thought you should know about it."

"Okay . . ."

"The picture you showed me, that boy with the messed up ear. I think I remember him. He was around in the neighborhood, went to school with my niece. I think his name was something like Kay or Kai. Something short like that."

I had braced myself, though I wasn't sure exactly what for (a torrent of abuse or perversity? An

obvious lie? A manipulative entreaty to help him in whatever way a college senior could?), but I wasn't expecting actual, potentially useful, information.

"Thank you," I managed. Not words I ever thought I'd utter to Darrin Parris.

I heard him breathing on the other side of the phone; I wondered if I was supposed to hang up, but then he spoke again. "The one who killed all them kids . . . I don't think he stopped. Not unless someone made him."

I wasn't sure how to respond to him, and a series of reactions flickered through my sleepy brain: the gall he had, the fact that he was right. Was I officially helping him now? What did it mean if I was? From this soupy mess of feeling, a single image emerged. A school photo of Shari Manners that I had found online, her braids clipped off with colorful alligator barrettes and her right front tooth slightly overlapping her left. Her shirt with a unicorn drawn on it in swathes of blue glitter. If she had lived, she would be just a bit older than me

now. We might have been classmates, friends even. Instead, she was in the ground, twelve years old for the rest of time.

"I think you're right," I told Darrin. "You can't fix evil."

6

Kie Wilkerson

August 21st, 2000

Outside the library, I checked my watch. Sundown was in about three hours, and for the second time in a row, I had nothing. I had a feeling that wasn't going to be okay. That white girl was always telling me that I didn't have to be scared, that we weren't doing anything wrong, and that I was just helping out my friends, but I don't think the big dude was on the same page.

He was even bigger than my Uncle Billy, and he cut his hair real close like an Army guy. It was so short that you could see how knobby his head was and how pink. It looked like little baby mice do

before they get fur on them. He had a gun, too. I'd seen him wear it and I don't think he cared if I saw.

You don't need a gun to help out friends. You need a gun when you're doing scary shit. That's what my mom's old boyfriend Trey told her that time he brought over a handgun and had her tape it up under her bed, just in case. She did it, too.

I was scared of the Army guy but I couldn't help but feel a little glad when Shari's uncle told her she couldn't go nowhere tonight. It never felt the same with a girl—it never felt exactly right. Shari had come to me, though, 'cause she heard from someone else that I knew how to get cash pretty easy. She wanted money, she said, because she and her big sister were gonna run away. They were going to go out west to L.A. and her sister was going to be a singer. She had a real good voice, I guess, and all they needed was a little bit more for both bus tickets.

She'd been asking me and asking me, and I tried to tell her that it wasn't fun, that she wasn't going to

like it, but she said she could take it. I didn't know about that. Girls are different, softer, sorta. A guy can sit through some stuff, do some stuff, and put it away inside his head. Girls are always feeling everything and crying about it. I didn't want Shari to get hurt because of something that I did.

When I told her that, she just laughed at me. "You think no one ever messed with me before?" she said. I hadn't. Shari was always sorta quiet. I only knew her because we were both in the slow reading group. I got sent there because I hated just sitting around and looking at a book—it felt like something was buzzing, tingling away in me and it kept pulling my eyes other places. Shari was there because the letters were always jumbled up for her, she said.

That was last year, though. This year Shari said she wasn't allowed to be in the slow group anymore because her uncle didn't want people thinking she was retarded.

"I might be, though," she admitted to me. "I'm the worst one in my class now."

I didn't know of anyone who wanted to get with her. Not because she was ugly or something but just because, half the time, people didn't even know she was there. If she was doing stuff, she wasn't doing it with anyone from school.

Shari told me that she could keep a secret "better than anyone, I bet." And to prove it, she wouldn't tell me where she'd heard about what I was doing. When I picked people, I tried to pick ones who wouldn't say anything and usually, they didn't. A few times, they'd even gone away after I'd taken them to the girl and Army guy.

Luka, André, Alysia, I never talked to none of them again after they went to see the white man in the house by the lake. At first I figured it was because they were mad at me. Like they thought it was going to be something other than what it was. Afterwards, they blamed me and didn't want to talk to me. Now, though, I was starting to think that something else was happening . . .

Which made it even better that Shari couldn't

go. But I still didn't want to show up with nothing tonight. They might make me go back to the lake house again. I hadn't been there in weeks, and I didn't want to go back, not if I could do something else.

Bringing another kid was a much better way to get paid. But how was I supposed to do that when school was out, and I'd already talked to almost everyone I knew? I stared into the library while I thought about it, staring at the big long table in front of the window where a bunch of kids were playing one of those card games.

At first, I didn't even notice the one on the end waving at me. He was the smallest at the table, and he had this big, desperate grin on his face, like he'd just spotted his mom or dad after thinking he'd lost them forever. I squinted at him, trying to figure out how he thought he knew me.

Then it hit me: he was in my class at school last year. Isaac or something? I remembered him because for about a month last spring he got kinda famous

in class for being really good at drawing animals that looked like people. For a little while, everyone wanted him to draw them as a tiger or a wolf or whatever.

I found myself waving back even though I wasn't at all sure that's what I wanted to do.

*　*　*

The way I saw it, everybody had to do stuff for money. Some people cleaned toilets, some people were teachers, some people sold things they made. It wasn't so bad; most of the time it didn't even hurt and I could just think about other stuff while it was happening to me.

The guy at the lake house wasn't mean or anything. He never yelled and he didn't want to knock us around, just do stuff to us or sometimes have us do stuff to him. He kept all kinds of junk food in the kitchen there, and he let me eat whatever I wanted. He had the good name brands of

everything, and sometimes he only wanted me to talk to him or to sort of lay with him on the sofa, and he still paid me for those times too.

It wasn't like it had never happened to me before, either. When I was little, Mom's boyfriend Trey used to try that kind of stuff sometimes, when Mom wasn't home or whatever. And Trey was a good guy; Mom said so. He loved us and he was taking care of us, that's what she said.

When Trey left, I was really sad because Mom was so sad. She almost lost her job because she couldn't go into work for three days. I wondered a lot then if it was maybe my fault that he went away. I never knew what I was supposed to do when he would touch me like that, and maybe I made him mad or something.

It wasn't too long before I went to live with Auntie Glory, and I thought that maybe Trey leaving was part of the reason. If he had stayed, Mom would have had enough money to keep me, I think.

Mom said that she couldn't take care of me right

at that moment, and that was why I had to live with Auntie. So I looked it up on the Internet, and I found out that it costs about a million dollars to raise-up a kid. I figured I could probably get away with a lot less than that because I didn't really need stuff like college or a car or anything. If I could save $20,000, maybe Mom could afford to take care of me, and I could go be with her again. I didn't want to tell Auntie, though, because I was afraid it would hurt her feelings.

Isaiah—it turned out his name wasn't Isaac after all—barely even asked about the money. He didn't want to know how much or anything. Mostly, I think he just wanted to go along with me. He was trying to tell me something about his sister, about how she didn't want to play with him anymore, all through the bus ride out of town, and I could already tell he wasn't the right kind of kid.

"Iz,"—he really seemed to love it when I called him by a nickname—"do you ever hang out with grown-ups?"

Isaiah shrugged and furrowed up his forehead. "Mama and Dad? Or do you mean like my teacher?"

"No, I mean like a grown-up who is a friend. You got any friends like that?"

He just shook his head at me. He was awful young, too. He told me his age, and we weren't that far apart, but he just seemed so much younger. The longer that bus ride went, the worse I started to feel about everything. It was like there was some kind of awful, burning stuff pooling in my belly, and it was eating me slowly from the inside out.

The worst part about doing the stuff I did was probably the dreams. I'd just turned eleven; I wasn't a baby and I hadn't wet the bed since I was three. But then I started to have these dreams where I was all "locked-in" and I couldn't ever seem to wake myself up, no matter what happened. I could feel it, that awful warm spreading feeling of the pee on my legs but I couldn't pull myself out of the dream, no matter how hard I tried.

Auntie thought that I was doing it on purpose, and she was always getting after me for being too lazy to get up and go to the bathroom. I couldn't tell her about the dreams. Once or twice, I had tried but it all started to come out wrong, and when I looked at her face, I knew she was trying really hard but that she didn't understand.

"Do you watch Pokémon?" Isaiah asked me as the bus turned on to Harper Avenue and headed away from the houses and stores. I shook my head. "Do you want me to tell you about it?"

I nodded. Isaiah brightened and I let the sound of his voice fall over me, like I was gonna drown in it.

•   •   •

The bus didn't stop right at the cemetery; we had to walk about a quarter of a mile. The bus ride had been really long and it was dark by the time we got off. I could tell Isaiah didn't like the dark because

his hand kept finding mine, and it didn't seem like he even knew he was doing it.

"Tell me more about those monster things," I said, trying to keep him happy.

"Um. Well. When they evolve, they sort of turn into these . . . "

His voice was a little shaky, like he was thinking about starting to cry. I wondered if he had the same feeling of wrongness about all this. Toward the end of the ride, he had started talking more and more about how he had to get home because his parents were going to be mad at him.

I realized that he didn't really understand what we were doing, not at all.

We walked along the edge of a gravel road until we reached a long, low stone fence that went all around the cemetery. Isaiah stopped short at the gate and looked up at me, his eyes so big they reflected some of the moonlight. "We're going into a graveyard?"

"Yeah," I said. "That okay?"

Isaiah nodded but it clearly wasn't okay. "You afraid of ghosts?" I asked him, smiling like everything was going to be just fine.

"My mama always makes us hold our breath when we drive past a graveyard," Isaiah mumbled, looking at his feet. "Are we gonna be in there a long time? Because I can only hold my breath for one minute. I practiced at the pool all summer."

It suddenly felt like there was something in my throat, like I'd tried to swallow a popsicle sideways. When I spoke, it even sounded creaky and painful. "Isaiah . . . you ever do any sex stuff?"

He shook his head and kept looking down. He was afraid, but I wasn't sure if it was of me, of this place, or of what his parents would do when he got home so late. Maybe it *had* been bad luck, after all, that Shari couldn't come? Maybe it would have been better if she had.

"A grown-up never messed around with you? Touched you or had you touching them?"

Isaiah shook his head again, mute with

discomfort. He was so little. He was only in my class because he'd skipped a grade. A smart kid. A young kid and there wasn't nothing wrong with him. He wasn't like me or even like Shari. There was so much bad shit he didn't seem to know about, and standing there in the cold and the dark, I realized that I didn't want to be the one to tell him.

"Listen," I said, crouching down and getting right in his face. "You wait here by this fence. I'm gonna go talk to some people, and then I'm gonna come back and we'll catch the bus home."

"No money?" Isaiah asked, looking up for the first time. He had a creeping hopefulness on his face, as if he didn't even dare to imagine that we might just go home safe.

"Not tonight," I told him. Maybe not ever again. I had almost $8,000 saved up. That was enough to go back to Mom's house, at least for a few months. Maybe I could get another sort of job. We could figure something else out.

"Now, what are you going to do?"

"Wait right here," he parroted back at me.

"Good. Don't come running in trying to find me, either. I might be a little while, but I'm coming back." He looked up at me with a real serious face, like he was noting down everything I said while I said it.

I made him crouch down behind the wall on the off chance that the Army guy went by here—they always came from the other direction—and then I started into the graveyard. As I went, I practiced what I was going to say out loud. I decided to keep it as close to the truth as possible. Lying was always easier when you didn't have to remember too much.

"I had a girl," I muttered to myself, "but she couldn't come at the last minute . . ."

When I climbed the hill where the old stone crypts sat, I could see their long, fancy car parked down below, half on the grass. My legs had started

to tremble just a little, but I didn't think it was from climbing the hills.

I looked over my shoulder one last time, and I was glad to see that Isaiah was hiding good. In the darkness, even I couldn't tell that he was there.

7

The Sculpture Garden

That morning class I skipped was actually the only class I had the next day, and when I asked Sammy if there was anything he had to get back for, he just gave me an "are you being serious right now?" look. So it was easy to take a little detour to the library, just to check on Mom's information.

For the most part, what she told me was accurate. Nina Barrow, Clark Simcoe, and Justin Frank were all abducted and killed in Sherwin County in 1998 and 1999. Their bodies were found in a tight cluster less than fifteen miles from West Allertown. Like in Bogeyman killings, the children were strangled and

dumped, often after less than a day. Their bodies were devoid of any significant DNA or fiber evidence. Police had suspected that the Bogeyman was washing his victims before he dumped them, but the Sherwin County killer definitely was. Nina Barrow had been found with still-wet hair. She smelled, according to at least one article, like an unfamiliar shampoo.

"These are the kids your mom thinks are related to the Bogeyman murders?" Sammy peered over my shoulder at an old newspaper article, a black and white photo of Clark Simcoe with his soccer jersey and floppy blonde hair. When his body appeared, Darrin Parris was living with his elderly father in Chicago, more than 200 miles away.

"I guess. It's hard to find information on them. This is one of six articles I'd been able to find." There were a couple of big articles after the second kid went missing and then some notes when each victim was found, but that was practically it. Most of the articles didn't even link the cases together

or posit a perpetrator. It was honestly perplexing. Other than Justin Frank, whose father worked in an auto parts factory, these kids were all from middle-class, two-parent families, not the kind of victims the media usually liked to ignore.

"There are some comments." Sammy pointed at a button at the bottom of the page that expanded a shockingly long list of predictably argumentative comments from all the usual suspects. There was a semi-literate racist blaming "criminals sneaking over from the ghetto," a woman crowing about how much she loved her own children and how she would "castrate anyone who ever touched them," and a couple of people wondering idly if they "ever found the guy."

The most interesting comment had no replies, though more than fifty people had "liked" it: heard that kidfucker Heapf punched his own ticket. good riddance.

"Heapf? Like Heapf Library?" Sammy asked.

I forgot sometimes that he didn't grow up around

here; Heapf was just a name on a building for him. "The Heapfs were—are, I guess—this big industrial family. They did a little bit of everything and they've been around forever." Since the 1700s, I believed. Basically, the government kicked the Indians out, and the Heapfs moved in. Their original homestead had been around Sherwin County, and you couldn't swing a dead cat over there without hitting Heapf Road or Library or Memorial Garden. Even all the way across the state at our university, a quarter of the buildings on campus were built with Heapf money.

"Which one was the kidfucker?"

I shrugged. I didn't really know much about the modern incarnation of the family; they kept a pretty low profile, though sometimes you'd hear about them making some big donation or backing some ballot measure. Nothing, obviously, about molesting children had made it into the news that I saw.

I googled "Heapf family 90s" and came up with almost nothing: a few listings of board members,

an article about a major endowment, and then, six results down the page, a jackpot.

Cole Patterson Heapf, the only son and heir to what remained of the family fortune died in 2002. Just about six weeks, in fact, after Parris's first trial finished. The obituary was sparse and though his age was listed as twenty-eight, the photo provided was clearly a high school senior portrait. He looked unassuming with a startlingly long neck and a toothy smile.

"He looks like some inbred Bavarian prince," Sammy observed.

"The Heapfs *are* kinda the Hapsburgs of the Upper Midwest."

"This says he died after a long illness, though. Not suicide."

"I would imagine that would be something the family might want to keep out of the papers." And if anyone could keep a secret in this area, it would be the Heapfs. That seemed like a deep, deep rabbit hole, though, and I couldn't make Sammy hang out

in West Allertown indefinitely. "Just let me check my e-mail and then we'll head out," I said, though Sammy just shrugged. I wondered what he thought about this, how it felt to him. Was it an adventure? The investigation montage in a movie? Was Isaiah just a character in someone else's story?

I was surprised to see that Detective Peterson had gotten back to me right away. I had forwarded Darrin's information to him from my phone that morning, though I had described it as "local gossip," rather than admitting that I'd seen Darrin in prison. Detective Peterson seemed energized by the tip but also frustrated:

> Got a record of a report involving Keith "Kie" Wilkerson in West Allertown but can't find a copy. Looks like the PD over there isn't digitized. If you are still in the neighborhood, could you go check it out? You can use my badge #.

I could feel my heartbeat pick up as I read the

e-mail. There was some thrill to it, some sense of puzzle pieces falling into place, but there was also the familiar low-level anxiety that bubbled up inside me when I faced the prospect of entering a police space. Especially the West Allertown police. Detective Peterson was one thing; he met me as an adult and a professional and he engaged with me on those terms. The West Allertown PD were the men and women who had loomed darkly over my childhood, the bogeymen before The Bogeyman. They were the ones who hassled my friends when they walked to and from school, who brought in older boys—cousins, brothers, classmates—for bookings with road rash on their faces, black eyes, broken bones. They were the ones who stood beside the car and peered suspiciously at my middle-aged, English-teacher father like they were facing down the Unabomber.

"You want me to come with you?" Sammy's voice startled me out of my anxious reverie. Sammy didn't have the same associations with the police

that I did, but he must have sensed something of what I was feeling. "C'mon," he grinned, "East Asian is, like, next door to white as far as the po-po are concerned."

It wasn't really true, but Sammy probably would be a lot more comfortable in the station than I was, and that seemed like something worth having. Another arrow in my quiver, I supposed.

As we walked out of the library and into the pounding sun, I wondered when I had started thinking of this as a battle.

* * *

The desk officer was a black man probably only a few years older than me. I wondered if I knew him or maybe his siblings. If he was local, he probably knew me, or at least knew of me. You'd think it would relax me, walking in and seeing a face that looked more like mine than like Cole Heapf's, but I knew better than that. I remembered my father

shaking his head over dinner one night, recounting the story of one of his students who was going down and would probably serve serious time for less than an ounce of weed. His mistake, Dad argued, was not being careful enough with the arresting officer because she was black, a girl from the neighborhood.

"He thought she was safe, that she understood." Dad shook his head sadly. "But as soon as she put on that police uniform, they became her people. That's who she'll protect."

I had thought about that conversation a lot over the years. Especially after I decided to get my criminology degree.

The man at the desk smiled at us. "Can I help you?" he asked, like a hotel concierge.

"I'm a criminology student. Detective Peterson at the Mt. Clare Police Department sent me to look up a file." I drew my credentials around me like a suit of armor, hoping that invoking my major and Detective Peterson would lend me some small degree of authority.

The young man looked confused. I noticed his badge read "King." I went to school with a Joelle King; a sister, maybe?

"You got a case number?"

"Just a name. Keith Wilkerson. This would have been about ten years ago."

Officer King rolled his eyes with relief. "Oh yeah. Of course. None of the old stuff is in the computer system yet. I've been begging them to go back and put those records in, but you know, funding is tough." He picked up the phone on the desk in front of him and punched in three numbers.

"Sharon? Yeah, I got a request here for an old one. Wilkerson comma Keith. Around 2000, I guess." He gave us a sympathetic look while the person on the other end (Sharon, I supposed) answered him. "Okay. Okay . . . okay." He put the receiver back down.

"Should be just a minute. Y'all want a coffee or something?"

I exchanged a slightly bewildered glance with Sammy. "Uh . . . no. We're cool."

I wondered if this was part of some kinder, gentler West Allertown PD, or if it was this specific guy, trying desperately to prove to me that he wasn't what Dad would have immediately presumed him to be.

Sammy and I retreated to a row of hard plastic seats. Without really thinking about it, Sammy reached out and took my hand. I let him.

* * *

"Looks like this is a custody thing. That what you're looking for?" Officer King asked, flipping through the thin manila folder that the unseen Sharon eventually provided for him.

"Yes." I tried to infuse my voice with certainty, though I had actually been expecting something like a missing person's report. I was afraid, though, if I

showed hesitation, that Officer King wouldn't let me see the file.

"Well, there's not much to it but have at it." He spun the folder across the desk at me.

Kie was a local kid but also he wasn't. He moved here around '99 to live with his mother's sister. The woman already had three children, and they lived in an apartment complex just four blocks away from Mom's apartment. The woman's name was Glory Green, and she was the one who had come in to make the report which, as I looked over the file, seemed like it might actually be a missing person's report after all. It was a "custody issue" only in the sense that Glory suggested Kie might have been lured to California by his grandmother—Glory's mother. Glory thought the woman was abusive and pointed out that she was Kie's legal guardian.

The officer had apparently been interested enough to follow up with the grandmother, who claimed that Kie was not with her, and she had not seen him in two years. But that was where it

ended—no listing Kie a missing person, no interviews with friends or relatives, no searches at all.

A small notation in a different handwriting listed the dates of the six other times Glory had called or come into the station in reference to Kie.

"Do you know why this wasn't followed up on?" I asked, spinning the file around and pointing at the list of dates. "This woman was really . . . tenacious."

Officer King looked uncomfortable. "There was a sticky note on the file when Sharon found it. Apparently the officer who interviewed Ms. Green felt she was . . . strongly motivated by the federal stipend for foster kids." His voice didn't change, but I noticed how he looked studiously downward at the file and not into my eyes.

I didn't ask him again. We both knew why no one had gone looking for Kie Wilkerson. It was the same reason my parents had to beg the police to look for Isaiah, at least until he was added to the Bogeyman's tally. They might not have said it in exact words, but we heard it loud and clear: *You're*

lying, you're over-reacting, you're in denial about the rebellious young thug you're raising. Your missing black child is not an emergency or a crime, and it's not even unusual. It's just the way things are supposed to be.

"This says there's an attached photo," Sammy read over my shoulder. "Shouldn't that be in the file?"

Officer King flipped through the scant few pages as though we hadn't just read them all. "Um . . . not sure. If it was a loose photo, it might have fallen out."

I bit back a snide comment about how that seemed unlikely, given the care and consideration with which the West Allertown police had treated Kie Wilkerson and his case.

"I can ask Sharon to have a look for it, but it might be faster to go to the source," the officer continued. I raised my eyebrows at him. "Ms. Green," he explained. "She still lives in Gravely, same apartment too. Her granddaughter works at the grocery store with my sister Joelle."

I couldn't help but smile a little. West Allertown was still a small world.

"You think she'll talk to me about this?"

"Oh, I'm sure she will." Officer King hesitated slightly. "You're Emerson Ward's girl, aren't you?" He said it like he already knew the answer and my nod felt almost superfluous. "Your brother—" he began awkwardly and I tugged on Sammy's sleeve and turned toward the door.

"Sorry," I said, "we're in a hurry."

* * *

"Someone reports a kid missing *six times* and the police don't investigate?" Sammy fumed while we waited at a red light a few blocks away from the station.

I was busy on my phone, texting Rona Miller who was tight with Joelle King back in the day and trying to get Glory's info from the granddaughter, who was apparently named Tina.

"Kie ran away a couple of times right after he moved in with his aunt," I said. "Just over to friends' houses, didn't even really leave town." But that's all it took for him to become a little delinquent in the eyes of the law.

"But even if he did run away, he was like eleven years old!"

Old enough, I thought, *around here.* When I was that age, I was already getting catcalls, already had clerks looking at me sideways when I lingered in front of a display at the store. Boys my age were already getting picked up by police. Everything they did looking like a drug deal or a burglary in progress. I remembered what Darrin Parris had said about his poor little niece: *she was grown.* For too many of us in this place, real childhood was a luxury and not a right. My phone beeped cheerfully. A text from an unknown number.

this is tina. gramma can mt w/ u 2 PM @ sculpt. gardens

And then, immediately following it, another beep.

u found kie?

For that question, I had no answer.

• • •

"I used to roller skate here," I told Sammy as we walked under the Sculpture Gardens entrance arch—HEAPF in big, wrought-iron letters. I'd never thought much about it before. "It was perfect because it's got a concrete walkway, and you don't have to worry about cars."

"Didn't you have a skating rink?"

"Mom didn't like me going out there after a girl got shot in the parking lot." Who could have known it was actually the public library that we should have feared?

"This seems a little . . . grim for public art, huh?" Sammy gestured toward one of the statues, ringed by a scrubby, poorly kept lilac bush. It was made, as all the statues were, from what appeared to be

salvaged metal. It depicted a woman with very long hair made from a fall of sheet metal. She was twisted into a grasping posture, as though trying to pull herself up toward the sky. The metal had been allowed to rust at its natural pace, leaving the figure patchworked in dull red blotches.

I had never really thought much about the statues, the same way I didn't think much about the street signs or the trees or the apartment façades because they had always been there, just as they were now. Seeing the sculpture from Sammy's outsider perspective, I had to admit that there was something agonized about it that didn't seem entirely appropriate for an outdoor community space.

Sammy drifted over to read the plaque underneath the statue while I headed for a concrete bench that had been shaped into the form of a supine woman, her hair covering her face like a veil. A woman about my mother's age was sitting there, patting the baby that she wore in a sling across her body. I took this to be Glory Green.

"Andrea Ward?" she said, half-standing as I approached.

"Yes, nice to meet you." I extended a hand toward her and glanced down at the baby, who was sleeping soundly with a little thread of drool linking him to a button on Glory's sweater.

"Grandbaby," she explained. "I heard you got news about Kie?" Her eyes were big and sad and mellow. She seemed like the sort of person who talked slowly, moved slowly, but there was something antsy in her when she said Kie's name.

"Um. Sort of. I'm working on a . . . project and looking into some old records. Some cases that, maybe, weren't thoroughly investigated?"

Glory snorted. "Kie didn't get any kind of investigation. That police officer all but called me a welfare queen." She shook her head. "He deserved better."

"You think your mother was lying about Kie being with her?"

"I know it," Glory said. "She wanted to get her

hands on Kie since the day he was born. I guess she figured he was her chance to start over after we turned out so bad. Raise a kid right this time."

"If she was pushing so hard, how did you get custody?"

Glory adjusted the baby in its sling, a momentary tenderness tempering her anger. "My sister was a sweet girl, but she had a lot of problems. The biggest one was just having Kie way too young. She knew she couldn't take care of him and she knew what living with Momma was like. She was the one who insisted that I take care of Kie.

"But then Momma starts writing him letters and e-mails, telling him how if he moves out to California he can do as he pleases and have a dog, get a car when he's fifteen, all this nonsense. But Kie was eleven years old. What eleven-year-old wouldn't want all that?"

My stomach felt the same way it did when I was carefully ratcheted up the first hill on a roller coaster. Glory, I realized, believed that her nephew

was alive. He'd been taken from her, sure, but she had never imagined that he had been murdered and dumped like trash.

"You never thought that he might have been . . . you know, the Bogeyman was happening about that time?" I offered as gently as I could manage, like probing a diseased tooth.

"No way. Kie was too smart to get involved in that nonsense." She winced as soon as she said it, and I realized she knew exactly who I was, exactly what had happened to my brother. I decided not to point out that Isaiah was just about the shyest and most cautious child I'd ever known and it hadn't saved him.

"He was aware, is all I mean. Had his head on a swivel," Glory added, almost apologetically.

It was possible that she was right, that he wasn't the unidentified boy. All I really had was Darrin's memory of an inconsequential interaction with a child more than a decade before. There was no proof, but there could be.

"I was hoping that you had a picture of Kie I could take a look at? Maybe add it to his file?"

"You mean there wasn't one in there already?" Glory's face crowded over with ten years of helpless rage at the system that had failed her. "Motherfuckers," she spit, opening her purse with an angry jerk. Her wallet was packed with photos of smiling children. As she sorted through them, I could see individuals go from fat-cheeked babies to sullen teenagers to young folks with babies of their own. Finally, she found what she was looking for, and she handed it to me, a small school photo. "We didn't have too many of just him. He wasn't even with us for a whole year . . . "

I tried not to let anything show on my face. If I looked the way I felt, she would surely ask me what was wrong and then I would have to be the one who said it out loud and made it real.

The boy in the photo had a huge grin, two dimples, slightly tilted eyes, and a small malformation of one ear. A baby elf. Our nameless boy. He had been

called Kie Wilkerson, and he did have a family that loved him, that searched for him desperately, even when everyone they encountered told them to stop.

"Thank you," I choked out. "I'll scan this and add it to his file." I didn't know if it was cruel or kind, leaving her to believe, at least for a few more days, that her boy was still amongst the living.

"Anything," Glory said, "that might help you all find him."

I whirled around, afraid that I was going to start crying in front of her. I practically ran back over to where Sammy was still looking at the statue, meaning to drag him out of the garden as quick as I could, but he resisted.

"Take a look at this," he said. "This is weird, right?" He pointed down at the plaque, which identified the statue as being the work of artist Fern LaMont and, next to her name in parenthesis, Willa Heapf III.

8

Fern LaDuke, née Willa Heapf

August 21st, 2000

It was going to frost early this year, I could always tell. There was a kind of taste that the air got, sort of industrial like cold metal with just a hint of grease. Plus, it was barely sundown and I was already freezing my ass off in this graveyard.

Johan wouldn't let me turn the car on. He said that the lights would attract attention but no one came out here at night; that was why we picked this spot in the first place.

"If that kid doesn't get here in ten minutes, I'm going into the ghetto myself and dragging his ass

out," I grumped to Johan who looked the same way he always looked: blank as a stone.

"West Allertown isn't a ghetto," he said, as if that were at all the point. "And you wouldn't have the first fucking clue how to act if you ever found yourself in one."

That wasn't entirely fair. I was the one who found Kie, after all. Johan couldn't have done it; he looked like a bouncer or a pop star's bodyguard or just somebody who had probably killed people for money. An earnest young white lady though, that was something else entirely. I was the one who called his mother (or his sister or whatever she was to him) and told her that I was tutoring him in math and science, that it was part of an outreach project. She'd sounded so delighted on the phone. "Kie loves science," she said. "He wants to go work for NASA someday."

I remember that very precisely because it was the last thing I remembered before I drank two-thirds of a bottle of Armagnac and awoke to Johan shoving

his fingers down my throat. After that, I refused to talk to the parents. I sent notes when I had to (I was good at making them look professional using gold embossing paper from our father's desk) but I didn't want to hear any more about some kid's best subject in school or his dreams for the future.

My dream for the future was just to live through it.

"I don't think he's coming," I said, popping open the glove box. I thought Johan might have some of those friction-activated hand warmers. Instead, I found a bottle of hand sanitizer, a coil of flexible metal wire, and a pistol. "Jesus," I muttered, shutting the glove box again.

"We'll wait a little bit longer and see," Johan said. He always talked like that, never asking a question when he could issue a proclamation. He never bothered to wonder whether I wanted to be out here in the freezing cold, waiting for new blood to sate my vampire brother.

That was a thing you never saw anymore. Back in the '20s and '30s or whatever, if there was a

serial killer going around murdering, they wouldn't call him a "ripper" or a "slasher," they called him a "vampire," a "ghoul," some kind of monster. It made more sense to me. Not every killer slashed or ripped (did any of them truly "rip"?) but they all seemed to take something, some life-essence, from their victims to feed something inside of themselves.

Cole had assured me that he wasn't hurting the children. "Not any more than I have to," he said. But I wasn't a fucking idiot, despite what everyone seemed to think. I saw the news stories about all the missing kids. Mom and Dad were pretty good at keeping things quiet in the news, but even they couldn't stop the train from rolling once the count reached double digits.

I knew that if I had picked up on this, Kie certainly had as well. Most of the kids he brought to us were one-and-done deals. I barely interacted with them, except to load them up in the car, take them to the lake house, and wait. When Cole was done,

Johan took them away. He paid them and reminded them not to tell anyone what happened.

At least, that's what Johan told me he did.

Kie, though—Kie I saw regularly. Often enough to get a sense of his personality and that he was a smart kid. Smart enough to almost never let on what he was thinking and wily as well. That's what had made him perfect for us; he was a natural born salesman, but when that didn't work, he could trick kids too. Kie had to have known what was happening to the boys and girls in his neighborhood. I deliberately tried not to remember them, so I couldn't say for sure, but I was willing to bet that some of the missing kids were Kie's friends, people he had delivered to us.

I would get out if I were him. The little pocket change we gave them after every "appointment" wasn't so great that it was worth all of this. There was a part of me that almost hoped I didn't see Kie tonight, darting across the graveyard to meet us. A

part of me wanted him to run away from all of us and never come back.

I knew, though, that if Kie really did bail on us, we would just find someone else. Another kid, maybe slightly dumber but in all other respects identical. I had learned a long time ago that when you're just a little piece in a big machine, there's no stopping the machine. All you wind up doing is getting yourself thrown away and replaced with something shiny and new.

Maybe it was thinking too much about Kie, or maybe it was the faint leftover smell from Johan's tuna melt lunch, but I felt a lurch of nausea in my stomach. I swung the door open and leaned out.

"Hey!" Johan shouted. "Watch the dome light!"

I retched into the grass, bringing up the gas station hot dog and bottle of rosé that had been my lone meal for the day. Morning sickness was a crock of shit. I barfed in the afternoon, at night when I was trying to sleep, almost every time I drove anywhere and half the time after I ate anything. The

only time I *didn't* reliably puke my guts out was just after I woke up.

I had started to wonder if the baby could feel how much I didn't want it and all the little passive aggressive things I was doing to make it go away, like drinking just as much and smoking both cigs and pot and eating nothing but cheap, packaged crap. Maybe it was fighting back, in its own way. If that was the case, it really wasn't endearing itself to me.

I'd like to say that my parents would have flipped shit if they had known that I was pregnant, but honestly, I'm not sure if it would even register with them. Cole's problems had a way of subsuming everything else in the house. My little molehill would barely register next to his Mt. Everest.

If I said I wanted to get rid of it, Mom would call someone and make an appointment, I'm sure of it. I didn't even know who the father was, for fuck's sake (on the weekends I went wherever the party was, and I did my very best not to see or hear or know

just about anything). There's no way they would want their fifteen-year-old daughter to actually have this—let's face it, probably retarded by now—baby.

But I still hadn't pulled the trigger on that.

I had time. My periods only stopped about a month ago and I looked it up online. The thing was like the size of a walnut right now and looked more like a salamander than a child. I wasn't completely sure why I was waiting, though. I knew I wasn't cooking up the next Nelson Mandela or Albert Einstein in there; the Heapfs were a warped branch of a dying tree and if my kid didn't turn out like my brother, he'd probably end up being another one of his victims.

There was that thing, though, about kids. They almost *have* to love you, at least at first. They come out wanting you more than anything else in the world. I guess I think it would probably be nice to be loved like that, at least for a few years. It'd be hard to give up on that idea, even if I knew it wasn't real.

It would probably all get fucked up though anyway. Sometimes I just looked at my mother and I couldn't believe that there was really a time when I thought that she could—or would—protect me from anything. I couldn't even imagine being that small, that young, that dumb.

"Here he comes," Johan said, flashing his lights three times. That was how Kie knew it was us, as opposed to some other pair of creeps parked in the cemetery at night. Before he even crested the big hill with the mausoleum, I knew we were going to have a problem; there was just one little shape moving through the darkness. He hadn't brought us anyone.

"That's twice this month," Johan muttered, seeing the same thing I did.

Kie knew he'd fucked up. He was already apologizing when he reached the car and he didn't throw open the door and climb inside the way he usually did. "I had this girl," he said, "but her uncle said she couldn't go out on a school night. I was working

on her all week and she just told me today. I didn't have time to find anyone else."

"Get in," Johan demanded. The last time Kie had come to us empty-handed, Johan hadn't said much of anything; he had just left the kid out there in the dark, making it clear that no new blood meant no money for Kie. Kie slid into the backseat, and I felt a little jump in my stomach. Maybe I wanted to reach back there and push him out of the car. Maybe I wanted to tell him to run.

Maybe I just needed to barf again.

"It is bad to lie, you know that, don't you Kie?" Johan said. The dome light, which had flickered back on when Kie opened the door dimmed again, and we were all just sitting there in the darkness.

"I know," Kie spoke slowly, like he was trying to suss out exactly what Johan wanted to hear.

"So you wouldn't lie to us, right? Because we've always been straight with you."

Kie didn't answer, so Johan turned around in his

seat. "Haven't we?" he demanded, way too loud in the little car.

"Yeah," Kie admitted.

"We told you what we needed and we told you what we were offering, didn't we?"

Kie's pause was about as pregnant as I was. "You didn't tell me . . . " he started before trailing off into wounded silence.

"Didn't tell you what?" Johan was talking too loudly again. I fought the urge to put my hands up over my ears. I used to do that all the time as a kid, a way of shutting out at least part of the world, at least for a little while.

This time, though, Kie wouldn't be bullied into answering. "Nothing," he said, almost sullenly, and maybe that's what made Johan do it—like if he was actually mad about the kid giving him lip or whatever. I'd never seen Johan be like that—doing stuff out of emotion, I mean. He got paid not to feel anything about anything.

Probably it wasn't anger at all. Probably, he'd

just figured out the same thing I had: that Kie knew Cole was hurting those kids, killing them maybe, and he wouldn't be bringing us any more of them.

And if Johan knew that, then he also knew that Kie knew what our faces looked like—Cole's too—and he knew where the lake house was. So I wasn't really surprised when Johan asked me to get out of the car.

What did surprise me was how heavy all my limbs felt, like someone had siphoned all of the blood out of me and piped cold lead into my veins instead. Just reaching my hand up to touch the door handle seemed impossibly difficult.

Kie reached for his handle in the back much faster, but he found the door already locked. Johan had probably locked it as soon as he got in the car.

"Get the fuck out of the car!" Johan shouted at me as, in the backseat, Kie started hurling himself at the door, kicking at the glass with his feet. He was a blur of limbs and sound, screaming things that

weren't even full words, and I just sat there, not moving, not even blinking.

All of this had happened so fast. Kie hadn't been in the car more than three minutes. Frustrated, Johan reached over me and opened my door himself. He gave me a single, brutal shove, sending me tumbling sideways out into the grass.

I landed hard on my hip. I threw out a hand to catch myself and slid wildly in my own puddle of vomit from earlier. I looked up at the car, where Kie had tried to climb over the seat in a desperate bid to get out my open door.

I saw his face, his eyes already streaming tears, as Johan put a hand on his chest and shoved him into the backseat. "Help!" Kie managed, just once, before Johan peeled off, leaving chunks of loamy turf behind him. The open passenger door was still flapping as Johan drove deeper into the cemetery, leaving me alone on the cold ground.

I laid there for a long time, rolling over on my back eventually to look up at the sky. Orion's belt,

the only constellation I could ever find. I decided that when I got home, I was going to tell my parents that I wanted an abortion.

I wasn't fit to be anyone's mother.

9

Carrying the Ghost

She was Fern LaMont on her personal website, Fern LaMont in the press for all her gallery shows, and Fern LaMont in the real estate records for her house in Sherwin County. The statues in the sculpture garden were the only place in the world where she was still Willa Heapf III, born 1984, the younger sister of Cole Heapf. She hadn't even been mentioned by name in his obituary and, as far as I could tell, that was her choice.

She couldn't completely rid herself of the Heapf connection, though. Her statues appeared not just in the West Allertown sculpture garden but also in and

around numerous other Heapf-related buildings, from libraries to colleges to business offices. Even the studio she kept on the edge of Lake Brighton had once been the Heapf family's summer house. It was less than thirty miles from West Allertown.

Sammy seemed to accept that we were going without my saying anything, though I myself was far from certain. "She probably won't even talk to me," I said. I wasn't even sure what I'd ask her if she did.

"You've come this far, Sherlock, don't stop now."

I slid into the passenger seat. "Does that make you my Watson?"

He smiled. "I'm gonna write about all your exploits." There was a part of me that wondered if I should be mad, if I should demand he not take this so lightly. But the largest part of me felt only gratitude. Everything about Isaiah was heaviness and darkness and shame. This was the first time in years that when I thought about my brother I felt . . . hopeful.

Sammy turned up the radio just loud enough so

we wouldn't have to talk. I rolled down the window, and for a minute I could pretend that we were just out for a drive in the fine fall air.

* * *

The house at the edge of the lake had once been very nice. It was still nice now, still huge and surrounded by acres of wild, undeveloped land, still with a porch that jutted out over the water, and if you wanted to buy it, it would still probably cost you a cool million. But it was different from what I imagined it had been in its heyday.

No one had bothered to do the usual kind of upkeep such houses required. A couple of the windows were broken and it looked like they'd been that way for years. That big porch was scarred and blackened from a fire that looked like it had effected most of the top story. The porch was serving as some sort of weird outdoor storage space now. I spotted a refrigerator, a canoe, and a huge bale of

barbed wire. The yard was littered with even more large pieces of metal, everything from car bodies to sheets of steel flooring, and a handful of goats moved freely about the property, moseying between the debris and chomping disconsolately on the uncut grass.

"Jesus," Sammy said when we pulled in, "this place is like an episode of *Hoarders*."

"She's an artist. And a rich person. So she's doubly allowed to be crazy."

Right outside the front door were what I took to be the "for sale" art. One sculpture, made mostly of rebar, was just a hand clenching tightly in on itself. I rang the doorbell and a chorus of barking dogs greeted me. Across the lawn, a lone goat looked up to see what the commotion was about.

I heard a female voice shouting. After a moment, the door swung open and a woman appeared. She looked older than I expected. I knew from my research that she was only in her mid-twenties, but I would have pegged her a solid ten years older than

that. Her face, especially the area around her eyes, was shot through with broken capillaries, and she had deep grooves next to her mouth. Her eyes were very light blue—so light, in fact, that they reminded me of jeans bleached in the laundry. She was wearing a kerchief over her hair and there was a scorch mark on her jeans.

"Fern LaMont?" I asked. She looked the two of us up and down, clearly presuming that we could not possibly be there to buy one of her undoubtedly over-priced pieces.

"Yes," she said warily.

"My name's Andrea. I'm a student at the college, and I was wondering if I could get an interview with you about your work?" I had developed this story on the way over, thinking that someone who changes their name and scrubs away any link with their family probably wasn't going to be too keen to talk about them in detail.

"I have a publicist. Number's on my website."

"Yes, I know. But I was hoping to get a more

candid, intimate type of interview. This is for my senior project, it's sixty percent of my grade." I was laying it on pretty thick but my desperation to talk to her was very real.

"What about him?" Fern asked, peering at Sammy skeptically.

"I'm her photographer," he said smoothly. "We were hoping we could get some shots of your art for the project."

She perked up a little at that and even gave Sammy a sliver of a smile. He was good at making people feel good about themselves. "It comes from being a chronic disappointment," he told me once. "I learned how to soften the blow."

As soon as I got inside, a motley pack of dogs swarmed around our knees, sniffing eagerly. "Hey, hey, get off." Fern waved her hands at them.

I was right about the house having burned at one time. There was a staircase that led up into a black skeleton of damaged beams, and I could smell the char, though it probably happened years ago. The

house's big central room was packed with furniture and with more assorted bits of metal. There were several broken bicycles, two washing machines, and more of that barbed wire. Fern had cleared a tight, single-file path to a series of dilapidated sofas that would have looked at home in a particularly slovenly frat house. She led us through her maze in a line: me, Sammy, and all the dogs like the world's lamest parade.

I took a seat on one of the couches, sinking down until I could feel my ass hitting the wooden supports underneath. Sammy plopped on the floor, taking a small terrier's head in his hands and scratching the little guy's ears vigorously.

"How did you find me?" asked Fern, who was apparently not too familiar with how interviews were supposed to work.

"I . . . the sculpture garden." Taken by surprise, an honest answer spilled out of me. "In West Allertown. I was fascinated by your treatment of the female body. It's very . . . dark."

Fern nodded but didn't say anything. She just stared at me with those eerie, washed-out eyes. From my seat on the sofa, I could see into what was apparently the kitchen. There was a family-sized jug of tequila on the table, less than half-full.

"I was just wondering, you know, where something like that comes from? That darkness?"

One of the dogs (some kind of collie) approached Fern and rested its long snout on her leg. She patted him absently. "Who can say where any motivation comes from?"

"Well, most artists have some idea." I pretended to be plucking a hypothetical scenario from off the top of my head. "Like, from their childhood or whatever."

Fern's eyes narrowed. "What does that mean?"

"Well, like, some artists have interesting upbringings. And they use that, you know, in their work to—"

"You didn't come here to talk about art," Fern

interrupted. "You're one of them, aren't you? One of the families?"

Sammy looked up at me. He didn't say anything, but I could hear him all the same: *steady, you're okay.* I knew that I would eventually have to level with her if I wanted to ask her any real questions, but I was hoping to get a little further than a minute in. I swallowed hard and nodded.

"You're not the first," she said stridently. "My parents used to buy them off in packs. They had a special account set up. You're not being clever, coming out here with your little project story. *Interview.* Interview, my ass."

"It was my brother," I broke in. "His name was Isaiah Ward. They never found his body."

Something passed over her face, like a shudder or a fit almost, but then her expression hardened again. "I'll tell you what I told all the rest of them. My brother is dead now and that's fine by me. Whatever you want, you can't get it from him."

"Did your brother kill those children in Sherwin County?"

"My brother was never charged with any crime."

"That's not what I asked," I snapped. She seemed a little taken aback but she didn't offer up any more information. "Why did he move into West Allertown? How did he take the kids? Where did he put my brother's body?"

Fern stood up. "I told you all I'm going to tell you. You'd better go now."

I grabbed her wrist desperately. "The sculptures," I said, "the twisted women. They're about you, aren't they?"

Fern froze, her wrist in my hands in an oddly intimate tableaux. On the floor, Sammy was trying his hardest to make himself invisible, but I could see how his shoulders tensed up even as he rubbed the dog's face. Slowly, Fern withdrew her hand and returned to her seat.

"I'm not going to incriminate anyone. I'm not *testifying* here," she warned. "And I'm not going to

promise anything, but if I tell you about him, will you go?"

"That's all I want," I said. She gave me a flat look because we both knew that wasn't true.

The collie dog returned to her knee and she looked down at him, smiling just a little bit. Then she started talking and her smile vanished.

"I don't remember a time when my brother wasn't molesting me. Though I'm sure there must have been one. I don't think Cole would have had much interest in infants."

"I was a late-in-life baby. Cole was a teenager when I was born, and Mom was already in her forties. But I was planned. My parents were having troubles, and they imagined that a baby might unite them again. That didn't happen. Ironically, it was Cole and not me who saved our parents' marriage. As it turned out, they could only handle one family-destroying catastrophe at a time, and Cole's had a higher body count."

She cringed even as she said it and added

immediately: "I'm not saying anything, when I use those words. *Body count.* It's a turn of phrase, you understand?"

I tried to force myself to nod and managed a short, downward jerk of my chin.

"I wasn't the only one, probably not even the first. Just the easiest. He didn't care if it was girls or boys, whoever he could get his hands on." She wrinkled up her forehead. "It was like we didn't even really have genders for him, like we weren't fully human. He had a word for kids under twelve; he called them 'sprites' and he said they were special. He used to apologize after he did it, but he'd apologize for . . . for profaning a magical creature. Not for hurting me, a real person.

"My parents knew but they deluded themselves into thinking that it was a phase that he would grow out of. He didn't. He didn't leave me alone until I got my first period. It was like putting on armor. After that, when I was mad at him, I used to hang my underpants from his doorknob. He couldn't

bring himself to touch it after that until it had been 'disinfected' and he'd have to stay trapped in his room." She smiled and someone might have mistaken it for the gently nostalgic smile of a woman recounting childhood pranks.

"He was never smart about it because he was never afraid of being caught. He'd go around chatting up little kids in public, asking them to come with him to one of our houses. He went after our parents' friends' kids, though, and that was where it started to bite him in the ass. These were kids from rich families—not as rich as us, obviously, but people with resources. They could afford a legal battle and that's exactly what they did. Mom and Dad settled four of those cases before they hired Johan."

"He was from somewhere in Europe, and I think he used to work with one of those private contractor outfits. His job was to rein Cole in and, if he couldn't, he was supposed to do damage control."

" . . . damage control?" I repeated slowly.

"Pick out . . . better targets," Fern explained. "Kids who wouldn't tell their parents what happened. Kids with parents who couldn't do anything even if they did. He taught Cole to be less obvious and to choose his moment."

I could not control the look of disgust that must have been painted across my face.

"I know," Fern's voice was strained. "But that's how they thought. Protecting Cole was the most important thing. Way more important than some poor kids. If it makes you feel any better, protecting Cole was even more important to them than their own daughter."

It didn't, but I didn't say anything.

"I can't say for sure what happened in Sherwin County. Or West Allertown. I was only a teenager then." As she had told her story, Fern had more or less maintained constant eye contact with me. Now, though, she looked down at the collie dog and wouldn't meet my eyes. "But I know that Cole hung

himself in early 2002 and there were no more murders after that."

She shook her head. "All that effort and my parents lost him anyway. They got divorced the next year, too."

Her story had the cadence of a tale she'd told more than once, the kind of simplified narrative of a life that one might develop for therapy or some sort of program like A.A. I wondered how much of it was true and how much was missing from it.

"Did your parents know that Cole was killing children?"

"I didn't say that. I didn't say he killed anyone." Fern's voice sharpened. I just stared at her. "But my parents paid a lot of money to a lot of people *not* to know things, do you understand? They paid people to make the families and kids go away, to make jail and court go away, to make Cole's constant attempts to kill himself go away. They spent most of our fortune paying to pretend they had the life they thought they deserved."

The Heapfs had clung to ignorance like a life raft, but not knowing had been an anchor for my family. It was drowning us. "Where did he put the bodies?" I asked, leaning toward her.

"I was fifteen that fall. And I hated him more than anyone in the world," Fern said, not answering my question.

I had a file folder where I kept all the information we had about Isaiah. It was my own case file, I supposed, and I had a big eight-by-ten picture of him in there. I didn't have any of that now, though, so I had to look through my wallet, find my own sad little school picture of Isaiah, the only such photo that I kept.

"This is him," I said. "This is my brother. Did you see him with Cole? Do you recognize him?"

Fern was facing me and the picture, but I could tell by her eye line that she wasn't really looking at it. "I'm sorry for your loss," she said, as mechanical and cold as any of her statues. "I lost so much to Cole, so I understand—"

"But you're still alive!" I burst out. Sammy rested his hand on my knee, but I barely felt it. "Just look at him," I said. "Please, just look at him and tell me if you know, if you know what happened to him."

Fern closed her eyes and opened them again, now looking directly at the photo. Her face was completely devoid of expression. "Sorry," she said and I realized that she had no idea who any of them were. She couldn't have selected her brother's victims from a lineup. To her, Isaiah was just another anonymous face.

Just another nameless child.

* * *

By the time we got out to the car, I felt like someone had injected a gallon of coffee directly into my bloodstream. The anger overpowered me, I tried to open the passenger door but I couldn't seem to make my hands work.

"She can't do that," I muttered when Sammy

came over to help with the door handle. "She can't just leave us like that. Not knowing."

Instead of opening the door, Sammy wrapped his arms around me. He smelled just like I remembered, anti-dandruff shampoo and chlorine and a little whiff of weed. We moved back and forth together, just by inches, the world's slowest and saddest dance. I realized I was saying the same two things over and over again, choking them out between sobs: "It's not fair" and "it's not right."

• • •

To my very great surprise, I actually slept on the car ride back upstate. I awoke to Sammy shaking my shoulder in the parking lot outside my dorm. It was night now and I must have slept nearly the whole six hours.

I invited him into my dorm, and he made himself comfortable while I checked my e-mail. I'd texted Detective Peterson earlier about my meeting

with Glory and told him I would scan in the picture she gave me on Monday. He wrote back, telling me that the department had reached out to the family for some DNA to test against the unnamed child's remains.

I sat on that e-mail for a while, wondering what exactly I could say in response. "Be gentle with them," maybe? But I knew from experience that there was no good way to hear that someone you loved was dead. I just wanted someone in all of this to treat that family with kindness, if only once.

I also had a flurry of e-mails from Melissa demanding to know why Darrin Wade Parris was asking for my phone number. She sounded scared that I was planning on scooping her.

I've been working on this story all semester, she wrote in her last e-mail. You could at least do me the courtesy of giving me a head's up.

I didn't reply to that one.

I even had a message from my Media and Crime

professor. I had never missed a class before and he had written to check in with me.

Are you okay? his message said, and there was no answer for that either.

Sammy was sitting on my roommate's enormous bean bag, an inherently ridiculous thing that he somehow still managed to make look cool. I chewed on my lower lip. I wasn't exactly sure how to ask him what I wanted to ask him, but I barreled on anyway.

"Sammy, would you . . . " I tried to find the words. " . . . smoke me up?"

Sammy let out a startled laugh that he tried to stifle, turning it into a snort. "You sound like someone's mom," he said, smiling.

It was true. I'd never been one for mind-altering substances. I didn't even really like to drink and I was always lecturing him about his usage. But I wanted to feel dreamy and light. I wanted to laugh. To *want to* laugh.

"I won't *smoke you up*," he said, mimicking my

stiff and awkward delivery. "But I will stay with you. If you want."

That was, I figured, the next best thing.

* * *

Sammy lay beside me in my narrow loft bed. My roommate went home almost every weekend, so I wasn't surprised when she didn't show up. He wrapped his arms around my stomach and pressed his face against the back of my neck.

"Isaiah's gone," I whispered.

"Yes."

"And we don't know where he went."

"Yes."

"And we probably won't ever know." He tightened his grip on me. This was the sort of conversation he was always urging me to have when we were dating, the sort of thing he thought would help me *heal*. I didn't feel like I was healing, though. I

felt like I had ripped the stitches out of a wound and was bleeding again.

I remembered our last big fight, maybe the worst we'd ever had, though in many ways it wasn't different at all from the other fights. Sammy told me that I was stuck, living for my brother instead of for myself. He said I couldn't even tell what I wanted anymore because I spent so much time thinking about what I ought to do. I thought at the time that he had a point but that he also didn't—couldn't—understand my situation. My responsibilities were real, the debt I had to Isaiah was real. If I went back to swimming or transferred to art school, that debt wasn't going to just vanish.

Now, though, I couldn't help but think that the opposite was also true. I could major in criminology, I could spend my days studying the faces of the dead, I could give a name to them, but I would still be the one who lost *him*. And he would still be gone.

"Did I ever tell you why my mom liked you so

much?" Sammy asked, his voice raspy and low, right against my ear. I shook my head.

"Her parents, my grandparents, left a kid in China. A daughter. They had to run to Taiwan at the end of the war, lots of people did. Granddad was off with the Nationalist army, Grandma was home alone, and apparently the Communist army was sniffing around, asking, 'Where's your husband? When's he gonna be back?' All that stuff. The way Mom tells it, they were about a week away from getting two in the head in a field somewhere.

"Grandma was pregnant. She had two kids and a huge overland journey to make on foot. She would have to carry the kids and she couldn't carry them both.

"A lot of people did something similar. If it wasn't a child, it was a parent or a sibling. Husbands and wives. Mom told me that everyone always believed it would be months, a few years at the outside, before they would be able to go back to their homes. Grandma and Grandpa never went back.

"Mom was born in Taiwan, the youngest of nine kids, but she said it really felt like ten. It was ten whenever they failed or fell short of expectations. It was ten every lunar new year when they gathered together to count the years since they had seen their loved ones. It was ten on every graduation day and wedding and funeral. Every achievement had a shadow in it, every mistake had a warning.

"She liked you because she said you understood what it meant, carrying a ghost with you."

"Did they ever find out what happened to their little girl?" I was whispering, but my voice still felt too loud.

"No. Sometimes you don't get to know how the story ends."

●　●　●

I dreamt again that night of Isaiah. I remembered everything.

I woke up before Sammy and rolled myself

gently out of his grip, climbing down from my bed. Settling in at my desk, I selected a charcoal pencil from the tin package and used a hand sharpener to get a fine, precise point. The sun was already out; it made the whole room a sort of rose-gold color. Good drawing light.

I opened my pad to a fresh page and got to work. I sketched out a kind-faced man with large brown eyes that tilted upwards in a way that made him appear thoughtful. I gave him a strong, low-bridged nose and a rosebud mouth, just like his sister and his mother. I drew in a beard, a head full of dense curls. I gave him a smile that was a little shy but very genuine.

I had plucked the face from my dream—a man I knew to be Isaiah in the ways that all things are known without being told in a dream world. He had spoken to me in a language I didn't understand but I could hear his voice—a lot like Dad's.

The drawing didn't take much time at all. It was as though my hands already knew all the shapes and

shadows I needed to produce. When I was done, it was almost like it had come from somewhere else, like how mediums used to produce automatic writing, said to be transcribed from the spirit world.

I didn't believe in ghosts or spirits, but looking down at his familiar smile, I could not help but think about what my grandpa had told me about the dreams: *maybe he is saying goodbye.*

For the first time in a decade, it actually felt like he was going somewhere. Like this goodbye was for good.

I could have left then, gone out to the library and sent the promised scan of Kie's photo to Detective Peterson. Instead, I fished my cell phone out of my backpack and hit the contact marked "HOME."

"Mama?" I said, when I heard her sleepy voice on the other end of the line. "I drew something and I'm gonna e-mail it to you. I think you'll like it."

"Baby," she told me, "I always like the things you make."

10

Possibilities

After Kie left him at the stone wall, Isaiah did just as he had been told to do. He waited. And he waited and he waited and he waited. He waited as it got darker and colder and later. The little glow-in-the-dark numbers of his watch gave off a dullish green that he used to examine the grass and the stones underneath him.

He waited, even after a big car came screaming out of the other gate and tore off into the night. He waited so long, in fact, that he found himself falling asleep sitting up, leaning against the prickly stone of the wall itself.

It was only then that Isaiah attempted to follow Kie into the graveyard, taking the same route up to the hill in the center where the enormous stone mausoleums perched over the rest of the tombstones.

Perhaps he had an idea that Kie had gone inside one of what appeared to Isaiah to be little concrete houses. Perhaps he was merely curious about them, having never actually been in a cemetery before. Whatever the reason, he began by investigating the nearest tomb, which belonged to the Courtney family. The last Courtney to be interred there was Elias Courtney Jr. in 1974, and the tomb had not been opened since then.

Isaiah found the front door (or panel, rather, as it had rarely functioned as a door) was closed tightly against all entry. He tried to pry it open, but his fingers, small as they were, could not slide into the gap between the pieces of stone.

Being a clever and persistent boy, however, Isaiah circled the perimeter of the mausoleum until

he noticed a small, unblocked window high on the western wall of the structure. By climbing on a nearby gravestone, he could reach the edge of the window and, with some difficulty, pull himself up and inside the building.

Unfortunately, in an attempt to lift his body up and over the window sill, Isaiah overshot his mark and tumbled down towards the ungiving stone floor inside the crypt. He hit the floor hard, headfirst, and immediately there was darkness.

He had that one wild moment of fear when he realized that he had pushed too hard and was going to fall, and then there was nothingness. He drifted in something deeper than sleep, never feeling it as the cold and the dark came for him.

* * *

Or perhaps he did not go into the cemetery. Maybe he decided instead that he would go along the side of the road until he got back home. He

remembered, more or less, the route that the bus had taken out to the graveyard, and he thought he could retrace the drive.

The car that hit him was a 1994 Buick Park Avenue, the first car that Christopher Malik ever owned. Christopher himself was seventeen and sober, alone in his car, returning from his girlfriend's house late at night. His greatest sins were sleepiness and preoccupation with his radio, which couldn't seem to produce anything but static. He had been so intent upon fiddling with the radio, so unconcerned about the straight, two-lane road he was coasting down, that he didn't even notice he had drifted so far over that he was essentially traveling on the shoulder.

Isaiah heard the car approach. He was not afraid though. He was used to the cars in the city, cars that moved relatively slowly through cramped streets with stoplights every other block.

A 1994 Buick Park Avenue weighs more than three thousand pounds. Isaiah weighed fifty-eight

pounds. The car's front bumper came up to the bottom of his spine. The strike was immediate and overwhelming. Isaiah was pulled under the car, but he was already gone by the time he struck the dirt.

Shocked, Christopher Malik didn't brake for a long moment, nearly driving into a stand of trees next to the road. When he stopped the car and got out, he immediately saw the little body in his wake, and he started to cry. Big, ugly tears caught in his chest and his nose, so hard and angry that it nearly made him puke.

If you asked him later why he did what he did, he would not have been able to tell you. It was as though he had checked out of his body, and someone else had stepped in, just for the moment. Like the copilot who takes over when the pilot dies of a heart attack.

He ran to Isaiah where a glance confirmed that the little boy was dead. Using just the heels of his hands (so as to avoid leaving fingerprints), he nudged the broken body towards the edge of the

road, where there was a thick row of trees, a tangle of brambles all around their trunks.

He pushed Isaiah down into a groove in the earth underneath one of those trees and stood back to make sure that he was not visible from the road. In a flurry of desperation, he grabbed a bunch of sticks and brambles from the stand of trees and draped them over Isaiah's body. Then he attended to the tire tracks leading from the road across the soft dirt of the shoulder. He smudged them, first with his feet and then with his hands. By the time he was done, his face was slick with sweat and tears.

He was never able to remember exactly how he got home. The next morning he lay in bed way too long, examining the dark crescents of dirt under each one of his fingernails.

• • •

Or maybe he didn't do any of that. Maybe Christopher jerked the wheel a quarter of a mile

before the cemetery. Maybe he weaved slightly as he got back on the road and felt a swoop of adrenaline in his stomach. *Christopher*, he told himself, *you fucking idiot. You're gonna get someone killed.* But he didn't. He didn't even notice Isaiah when he drove past him because the boy was so small and walking nearly in the ditch, hidden by underbrush.

The next car to come along did notice him, however. The driver was a man in his mid-thirties, Raymond Firth. He had a precision-sculpted goatee and a spot on the state sex-offender registry. He spotted Isaiah right away and pulled over almost automatically. At first, it was a legitimate impulse, curiosity mixed with a sense of civic duty. What the hell was a little kid doing out there all alone at night?

Then, in the glare of the headlights, he recognized the boy. He was the one in the 7-Eleven earlier with that bossy girl. He hadn't done anything wrong, just tried to help out. He remembered what

it was like not to be able to afford all the things that the other kids seemed to have so effortlessly.

Maybe he didn't even intend to do anything. Maybe he genuinely believed he would only give the little boy a lift back home and leave it at that. Maybe he hoped that, this time, he would make the right choice.

Isaiah hesitated before getting into the car. He knew from his teachers and his parents and his sister that a kid must never get into a car with a strange man. But, as Raymond Firth pointed out, they weren't really strangers. They had already met at the store. Raymond even knew some of the same folks that Isaiah knew. And even Andrea would say that it was better to get in a stranger's car than to walk around alone at night.

Raymond drove off with Isaiah in the front seat and the very best of intentions. But Isaiah reminded him strongly of his own little cousin, the first real love of Raymond's life. As it had been so many times

before, the compulsion was stronger than any desire to do right by someone else.

Raymond Firth did not take Isaiah home—not to Isaiah's home, at least.

Later, he buried the boy in his own back yard in a spot he would eventually cover with a cement slab and a toolshed. He never moved out of that house— he never could. He and Isaiah would live there forever. Together.

*　　*　　*

But, then again, maybe not. Maybe Raymond Firth decided that, instead of driving back home, he would crash on the sofa of a friend in West Allertown. Maybe he never headed out on that long, dark highway at all.

Maybe Isaiah walked almost all the way back to West Allertown. By that time, his feet hurt and he was crying because he wasn't sure he was going in the right direction. Maybe he stopped at a

convenience store on the edge of town, hoping that someone there would let him use the phone and he could call his mom and dad.

Before he went into the store, however, he encountered a strange white man wearing motorcycle leathers. The leathers weren't black and tough like the ones Isaiah has seen on TV. Instead, they were white and red, and they looked brand-new, like this was the very first time the man had ever worn them. He imagined that he could hear them creak and crack every time the man moved.

The man's motorcycle was custom-painted white and red as well. Cole Heapf rode it everywhere because he never learned to drive a car. It was annoying, then, that Willa would call him in the middle of the night and demand that he pick her up at some ghetto gas station. That was supposed to be part of Johan's job: driving them around, getting them where they were going, getting them the things that they needed.

Cole Heapf knew that Isaiah was special the

moment he saw the boy's face, illuminated in the ugly yellow light from the gas pumps. It was perhaps the sprightliest sprite face he had ever seen. Those big, warm eyes had a steady, knowing look. Cole knew he was the sort of boy who would *understand*, the sort of boy who would forgive. And Cole Heapf wanted, more than anything else, to be forgiven.

"Hey, kiddo," Cole said, noticing how the little boy's eyes were drawn again and again to the motorcycle beside him. "You ever ridden one of these?"

Isaiah had not, and Cole figured that Willa could find her own way home. She was a grown girl, after all.

Later, when Johan had taken care of everything, Cole would get a soft sort of lecture about going out himself, about being seen. But Cole did not care. For a moment, at least, he had gotten close to something pure and bright. Something from the world before adulthood. Of course, he had spoiled it in the end. He always did. That's why Johan had to take them away—it was better than having them live as

they were, all ruined but still with the memory of what they had been before. That was how Cole felt all the time, and he couldn't imagine anything worse than that.

Willa was mad at him too (she ended up calling a cab), and she wouldn't speak to either of them all night. She just stayed in her room through the night and all the next day, the smell of pot creeping out from under the door. She was so boring now, and she became more boring all the time. Cole hoped he never got as old and boring as she was, though sometimes he was afraid, desperately afraid, that it was already too late. That he'd never be able to claw his way back to the world of the sprites, no matter how many he took.

He couldn't let himself think like that, though, because that kind of thinking was dangerous. He didn't want to hurt anyone, least of all himself.

●　●　●

Or maybe—just maybe—it was none of these things. That little boy, crouched in the darkness at the edge of the cemetery, holds all of these possibilities (and more besides) inside of him. He is alive and dead and every possible thing in-between, all at once. Schrodinger's Boy, he waits and waits for his fate to resolve into something sure and hard and certain.

Slowly, it gets colder and later, and Isaiah Ward might just wait forever.

AUTHOR'S NOTE

I t's hard to find a pithy nickname for a predator who targets the most vulnerable—and most
cherished—in our society. "Slasher," "Ripper,"
"Strangler," "Slayer": none of these seem quite
appropriate when talking about someone who stalks
and murders children. Perhaps that is why the media
so often defaults, in these cases, to the most baldly
descriptive, yet still disturbing, moniker: child killer.

In Michigan in the 1970s, he (or possibly she
or even they) was called The Oakland County
Child Killer, and he took at least four little lives
over the course of roughly one year. Like the

similar Australian predator dubbed "Mr. Cruel," the OCCK became infamous for his attention to detail and the relatively few pieces of evidence he left behind.

Violated in life, the children he killed were curiously fussed-over in death. Their bodies were painstakingly bathed and redressed in their own clothes before being left in public spaces to be discovered. In one particularly horrifying incident, the mother of one missing boy went on television to beg the perpetrator to let her son return to her so she could take him out for his favorite meal, Kentucky Fried Chicken. When that child's body was found shortly thereafter, medical examiners determined that his last meal, not even fully digested, had been fried chicken.

The Oakland County Child Killer was never identified, though there have been a number of theories proposed over the years.

There is a tendency for crimes against children to develop an atmosphere of conspiracy

theories around them. For example, the "Satanic Panic" fears of the 1980s almost always centered around the abuse and murder of children, and cases like Belgium's Dutroux Affair and the ongoing revelations about the Catholic church have sparked rumors of large, well-organized, and well-connected rings of pedophiles who regularly kidnap children to abuse and torture.

These sorts of theories often have some grounding in reality, in the sense that child molesters have been known to operate for long periods of time within closed communities, protected and sanctioned either by other pedophiles or by powerful friends. Consider the case of Britain's Jimmy Savile, a beloved television presenter in Great Britain who was allowed to abuse hundreds of children over the course of his decades-long career. Another case involved Australian murderer Peter Scully, who relocated to the Philippines for more unrestricted access to the small children he used to create pornography

for his thousands of "fans," watching from all over the world.

Stories of pedophile networks that reach into every arm of the government and police, however, are much harder to document, though such theories never fail to crop up in cases of multiple child murders. When it came to Michigan in the late 1970s, however, there might have been a little more reason for suspicion than usual. The investigation into the OCCK eventually led to the discovery of a loose coalition of several successful businessmen, who had started a charity organization for at-risk youth that they used to find and groom victims, much as Penn State's Jerry Sandusky would do several decades later.

It was a dramatic story involving money and power and isolated islands in Lake Michigan. Some of the most significant families in the state were rumored to have been involved in what turned out to be a nationwide child pornography ring, but actual arrests were few. Some alleged that it was

the money and power of these perpetrators that kept police and media from explicitly linking the Oakland County killings to what was going on further upstate. There was something so careful, so *organized* about those murders that it seemed like it had to be the work of some shadowy group with enough resources to keep the crimes unsolved even until today.

Oakland County is not far from Detroit, and it shares a lot of commonalities with the city. Both regions were historically dependent upon the automotive industry and both have risen or fallen according to the fortunes of companies like GM and Ford. But Oakland County did differ from Detroit in one important respect: it was white. Overwhelmingly so, in fact. When people talk about the "White Flight" of the 1960s and 1970s, they are talking about Oakland County or places much like it. As soon as that first child went missing in Oakland County, the people of Michigan were on high alert. The four missing children were seen as

everyone's children and their stories dominated the news cycle. For years to come, parents would invoke tales of the OCCK to remind their own offspring of "stranger danger" or explain why they weren't allowed to go to the park alone.

Just a few years later and a few states away, another serial killer targeted children and terrorized another community, but the ordeal wound up exemplifying some stark differences in the American justice system for black families.

In the late 1970s, Atlanta, Georgia was a *de facto* segregated city, and the police were definitely not seen as working for the black community. When young boys started to go missing from predominantly African-American neighborhoods, the police did not respond by launching investigations or organizing searches. Instead, they adopted a "wait and see" approach, presuming that these children were runaways who would get in contact with their parents eventually.

When young boys started turning up dead in the

same geographical area, police did not immediately assume the murders were connected. There were so many ways, apparently, that a black adolescent male might end up murdered and abandoned that it would be hasty to suspect a serial killer.

Everything went just a little bit slower in what would eventually be called The Atlanta Child Murders. The investigation erred on the side of presuming there was *not* a killer operating in the city. Police bemoaned the difficulty of getting information from a community that was historically distrustful of law enforcement. Families spoke out about being dismissed or ignored. Some of the first national news coverage focused on the discovery that Atlanta police were not even bothering to write down all of the tips that came through on the tip line, let alone investigate them.

By 1980, this case was rapidly drawing national attention. Perhaps stung by media criticism and with more than a dozen unsolved murders Atlanta

police refocused their efforts and threw their resources behind the search for the killer.

In the vacuum created by the lackluster police response, though, a number of theories had bloomed, flavored by the unique cultural and historical situation of the affected communities. Perhaps the most popular and enduring was that these abductions and murders were the first volley in a race war, an attempt by the KKK and other powerful white supremacists to destroy black communities by destroying their young men. In the same way that police being bribed or intimidated by a gang of wealthy and powerful pedophiles made sense to white, middle-class people in Michigan, the idea of the police standing aside while virulent racists enacted a campaign to demoralize and degrade black communities seemed entirely plausible to many people in Atlanta.

When the police finally identified a perpetrator, and he was a young black man native to the area, theories changed but the conspiracy element didn't

entirely go away. Some people thought the convicted killer (Wayne Williams) was innocent and was railroaded to avoid identifying a white culprit because authorities feared an inevitable backlash. The more likely version of that idea is that Wayne Williams did indeed murder some of the more than twenty people he was accused of killing. Fiber, DNA, and hair evidence recovered from some of the bodies makes a very compelling case for his involvement. Many people, however, believe that Williams is not the sole perpetrator and that some of the crimes included under the "Child Murders," may not even be related.

There is some evidence for this theory. The victims were bludgeoned, strangled, shot, and stabbed. They were boys and girls, children under fifteen and men who were nearly thirty. This range of victim types and methods of murder does seem to suggest that these crimes might not be the work of just one individual.

Officially, though, the Atlanta Child Murders

have been solved and the killer identified and jailed. If there is more to the story . . . well, we probably won't get to hear it. And that, really, is the crux of the issue. The murder of a child is something that most of us find unfathomable. It is very tempting to develop narratives to explain what appears to us as an impossible level of deviance. How could one person be so broken? So devoid of care and empathy for the most helpless amongst us?

No, there has to be *more*. There has be something extraordinary and remarkable because when the loss is so great; how can the cause be ordinary? The truth is, there's no such thing as a good or satisfying explanation for the murder of a child. Whether there is a name and a culprit, a narrative of what happened, or simply a sea of questions, there is no real *reason* that will ever truly bring closure to a family or a community. There is only the unknowing and the peace that folks have to make for themselves.